The Skeptics' Guide to the Mysteries of the Universe

JESSICA ARDEN

Ebook ISBN: 978-1-946188-01-4

Print ISBN: 978-1-946188-05-2

CONTENTS

For my family

Thanks for being there with me, every step of the way.

CHAPTER 1

Nothing calmed Julie Deveaux's nerves like showing chaos it was *not* the boss of her.

With that in mind, Julie grabbed her research notes and set out early for the big meeting with her graduate advisor. There was too much riding on this and Julie hadn't been able to hit a breakthrough on her thesis research, as she'd hoped. That could very well spell the end of her project, unless she could convince Miranda to give her more time.

She strode with purpose along her well-worn path through the French Market and down into the heart of New Orleans's French Quarter. Leading hundreds of ghost tours had armed her with an intimate knowledge of every street and haunt of the historic neighborhood, and impressive calf muscles to boot. She navigated past over-crowded streets and a seedy alley until she found what she was looking for.

Julie breathed in the scents of boiled crawfish, red beans and rice, and a hint of magnolia. They almost masked the funk of the standing water and the gutter punks feeding their dog on the curb. Locals and tourists alike bustled through, bobbing their heads to the notes from energetic trumpets wafting over from nearby. A feeling of homecoming stirred in her chest. Beneath the greenery that dripped from ironwork balconies lurked nearly three hundred years of history. Three hundred years of stories and scandals and lives. Testaments to a city—and its people—who'd survived fires and floods, hurricanes and yellow fever, and remade itself every time.

Some of the tension leaked from Julie's shoulders as she emerged into the heart of Jackson Square. Still fifteen minutes to kill before the meeting.

"Reading?" one of the street psychics called out to her. They were lined up two-deep with their camping chairs and velvet-covered milk crate reading tables between the St. Louis Cathedral and the park. Julie swerved to give them all a wide berth.

Not that she didn't believe in psychics, it was just that when it came to the future, she had it under control. First, she'd write the most glorious and provocative thesis on the Madame Sophia murders and graduate with honors. Then she'd get a history professorship and continue to help run the family ghost tour business. Well, provided that her thesis wasn't red-lighted at the meeting this afternoon with the recent impasse.

Her stomach turned over at the thought, but she had a mind like a stubborn puppy that wouldn't let go of a toy until it broke open, all secrets revealed. She'd sort it out. Somehow. There was enough tumult in life without a cryptic message from the "other side" throwing things off. Besides, the future was something you created and busted your ass for, not something you sat around waiting for after an enigmatic message about the river and the number three.

"You look like a girl who wants to hear about her true love," a psychic draped in ethereal yellow robes called out to Julie. "Only sixty bucks."

With an eye roll, Julie picked up her pace. That was problem number two with psychics. Even if she weren't on a student budget, she wouldn't buy what they were selling: namely true love and destiny and soulmates.

Before she'd made it out of the psychic gauntlet, a third medium called out to her. "You're right, you know." The woman's voice rang through the air, low and rich and filled with long southern vowels. "About Sophia. She didn't do it."

The hair on the back of Julie's neck prickled. "I beg your pardon?"

"That's what you're studying, isn't it?"

Julie eyed the older woman warily. The hand-painted sandwich board in front of her setup advertised Readings from the Beyond by Francine. The name didn't ring a bell, and Julie would definitely remember this woman if she'd seen her before. In her elegant suit and mink stole, which she wore despite the sweltering heat, she didn't look like the other street psychics in gauzy costumes.

"Sorry, do I know you?"

"No, but I believe I know a thing or two that might interest you." Francine gestured to the chair across from her.

Julie glanced toward the coffee shop where she'd meet her advisor, her stomach doing a nervous flip. This was hardly a credible primary source, but something—call it desperation—kept her from walking away.

"Did you know her?" Julie asked.

"A little. She was good people. She'd never get mixed up in the sort of things they locked her up for."

"Is this personal conviction or intel from the beyond?" Despite her better judgment, Julie sank into the offered chair and retrieved her notebook and pen.

Francine pursed her lips. "Let's call it the former based on the latter."

"So these other things that might interest me, what are they?" Julie pushed her long curls out of her face. Anything that pointed her to evidence she could substantiate could be the breakthrough she badly needed.

Francine's gaze moved to the sign advertising her reading rates, and she folded her arms over her chest. "Would you like a palm reading or tarot?"

"Is that really necessary? I want to know about Sophia, not myself."

"I'm afraid it's all terribly intermingled."

Julie groaned and gave Francine a skeptical frown.

Francine's gaze moved to the psychic set up under the umbrella next to them. At whatever she saw, her mouth quirked into an amused smile.

Curious, Julie followed her gaze and couldn't help admiring the view. A new client slid into the empty seat and flashed a smile at her. He pushed up the sleeves of his oxford shirt and leaned forward to chat with the psychic, his tall, lean-muscled body a bit too large for the folding chair. Chunky glasses lent a studiousness to his features, but not the library shut-in variety. There was also a challenge and restless energy to his movements as he studied the psychic across the table from him, as if he were taking in every detail, always researching, just like she was.

Francine cleared her throat, and Julie snapped back to attention.

Francine's eyes twinkled with mischief. "As I was saying, in your case, these factors are all related. Interdependent, even." From a velvet bag, she produced a deck of tarot cards. "What do you say?"

With a sigh, Julie glanced at her research notebook. There were so many questions about the Madame Sophia murders she burned to know the answers to. Conventional methods were getting her nowhere. She could take what she needed and ignore the rest, right?

"Okay. But if you say one word about 'true love,' I get a refund."

Deep rumbling laughter—definitely male—drew Julie's focus back to the attractive client at the booth next to theirs as Francine shuffled the cards.

He leaned back in his chair, white-blonde hair stirring in the breeze. "Okay, so what's in my future? Money coming my way by the boatload? Let me guess, also a side of fame and a gorgeous fellow history buff who gets my obscure X-Files references?"

Something about the playful skepticism in his voice curved Julie's lips upward. He didn't strike her as someone who'd normally visit a psychic. What was his story?

Francine tapped the cards on her velvet-covered table and shuffled yet again.

"You're being very thorough there," Julie said.

Francine made a noncommittal sound. "Sometimes it takes a while."

Julie leaned back and tapped her pen against her notebook. The sound of cards sifting together blended with the low notes of a brass band and the sound of History Buff's psychic explaining the significance of his tarot spread.

"And this one is in the past position." She tapped a card. "You've been struggling with your belief in someone who was once close to you. You believe this person double-crossed you and now you're trying to set it right."

A crease deepened between the guy's eyebrows. Something flashed in his eyes—pain?—like the woman had hit the mark. But after a fraction of a second, his skeptical smirk slipped back into place. His psychic continued through his present and on to his future.

"Yeah, but this one's inverted," he said. "That means recovery, an end of some phase or regeneration. Ooh, does that mean I'm going to grow a new arm if something happens to this one? Nice try."

A skeptic who knew his tarot cards. Interesting. Julie's puzzle-obsessed brain locked onto this intrigue.

"Ready to cut the deck, dear?" Francine held out the cards.

Time for Julie to get some of her own answers.

"There are three things you seek." Francine laid down the cards with a swick. "But only two you let yourself acknowledge."

Julie folded her arms over her chest and pressed her lips together.

"One to satisfy your mind, one your home, and one your heart."

"Yeah, I'm a regular one-woman cast of The Wizard of Oz." Julie shifted. "Let's focus on the mind, okay?"

Francine shook her head, but laid another card down on top of the first one. "The autopsy." Her eyes fluttered shut and she pressed a hand to her temple as though receiving some sort of transmission. When she opened them again, she cocked her head to the side and ran a finger over the Magician's raised hand on the card. "Look at what's left in the autopsy."

Julie's curiosity stirred. "Do you mean someone tampered it with?"

"Perhaps, but I don't think so. The message feels very specific. Look at what's left."

Cryptic, perhaps, but you never knew. Julie jotted a note.

Francine flipped over two more cards. "You're at a roadblock in all three areas. Ghosts of your past hold you back. There are walls where there should be open spaces."

Though this verged on personal, Julie noted this as well. She thought of the bedroom walls in her apartment full of unpleasant memories, but it would take a construction crew and $12,000 that she didn't have to make the renovations happen.

"And your research..." Francine touched the Fool card. "You're so close to answers that will change everything, but you'll have to work through your problems in the other two areas to make the leap you need."

Julie looked at the Fool walking blithely off a precipice. Great, a leap of faith—right off a cliff. Exactly what she needed.

"So what do I do?" Julie asked.

Francine settled back in her chair and fixed Julie with a knowing look.

"The grandson is the key. He could help you in more ways than one."

Julie's heart sank. She would go to almost any length to get answers, but she drew the line at sticking her fingers in the old wounds of those who had already suffered too much because of this situation.

"I didn't say it would be easy," Francine said.

"No, just unethical," Julie muttered.

"I doubt that'll be the case."

The Saint Louis Cathedral bells rang out over the square, ushering in the hour. Time to meet Miranda already.

Julie handed Francine two crumpled twenties before collecting her books.

Francine called after her: "You resist, but fix the home, fix the heart, and you'll get the answers you seek."

CHAPTER 2

Julie ambled dejectedly down Chartres toward the cafe.

Fix her heart and her home and the answers would come. Right.

Julie admitted her house could use some rehab. Her heart, on the other hand, was in mint condition, thank you very much. She'd made note of the patterns in this area as well. And thanks to her sensible, keep-it-casual approach, she wouldn't have to deal with a string of heartaches that were so much a part of her family history that she should probably report them on her medical forms next to angina and wheatgrass allergies. Things she also wouldn't have to worry about: guys running out on her and swiping her great-grandmother's china on the way out. She certainly didn't need this grandson swooping in to wreak havoc on her perfectly fine life.

There had to be another way to get to the bottom of th Madame Sophia thing.

She looked up to see three teenage boys sprinting down the street, howling with laughter. Before Julie had time to sidestep, one wheeled into her.

"Oof." Julie's research notes and books went flying into the street. She slammed into the person behind her and tumbled onto her ass.

"I'm so sorry!" Julie said, turning to see who she'd dominoed into. It was the skeptical history buff fresh from his own psychic reading, sifting through a jumble of papers, not all of them Julie's. Her vantage point on the ground gave her a rather nice view of his backside.

A few paces away, Julie spotted his chunky glasses. She snatched them up just in time to save them from a fate of trampling by tour group.

"Here. You might need these."

When he looked in her general direction, she pressed them into his hand and his shoulders relaxed after slipping them on.

"Thanks." His now-clear gaze fixed on her. His smile widened and green eyes danced in a way that produced a warm, fluttery feeling in Julie's chest.

They held each other's gaze for a heartbeat before he reached to help her up.

"Sorry about—" Julie flipped her hand around. "You know, crashing into you like a rogue bowling pin."

She looked down and pushed a strand of hair behind her ear. With his hand in hers, the rough callouses pressing into her palm, her pulse quickened, and she felt suddenly shy.

Maybe because she did most of her flirting under the cover of night and neon bar lights. Where she could call all the shots.

"Well, I guess that's one way to introduce yourself." He grinned and then bent to retrieve one of Julie's notebooks.

"Looks like our papers got intermingled here. Are you a student too?"

Intermingled—the word reminded her too much of Francine's words—*I'm afraid it's all terribly intertwined.* Julie tucked her book under her arm and kept her fingers busy sorting his papers from hers to quell the disquiet from that coincidence.

"Um, yes." She swallowed, feeling the familiar reluctance to share building up inside of her. "Working on my grad thesis. Hence all the notes," she said. "You?"

"Me too. At Tulane."

Julie handed him a hardcover that looked as beat up as her own.

"So, did you gather any insights from the beyond?" He wiggled his fingers in a mock-spooky gesture.

"More like frustrations from the beyond. What about you?"

"Nah. That lady was a quack. She probably skimmed Tarot for Dummies last week and then set up shop." He picked up the last of the papers.

Their eyes locked. Julie felt the tingle of attraction again. Something about it, with her caught unawares in broad daylight, felt dangerous.

She broke the gaze and worked her books and notes into her already overfull purse.

His gaze veered to her book. Eyes widening, he held up his own identical copy: The Skeptics' Guide to the Mysteries of the Universe.

Julie clapped a hand to her mouth. Part in-depth collection of New Orleans history and legends, part philosophical musing on all things un-knowable. This had been one of Julie's favorite research finds.

"That's been out of print for fifteen years. I think there were only ever 100 copies. How do you even have that?" she asked.

"I've got a friend at the used bookstore over on Decatur. She kept an eye out for me."

Questions swirled in Julie's mind. What exactly are you studying? Are you as obsessed with folklore and legends as I am? Are you dependent on and terrified by things unknown? Does that book make you stare down the most uncomfortable parts of your soul?

But asking those questions would mean divulging her own answers, giving away parts of herself. Doing that would mean getting deeper into something very, very unknown.

"Hey, do you want to get some coffee?" he asked. "We can discuss the finer points of the human experiments in the LaLaurie mansion."

Julie's heart gave a nervous stutter, but—God help her—she found herself wanting to push past it. Even if it was partly to give destiny the middle finger by flirting with this hot, non-grandson history nerd. Who's in charge now, fate? I am, that's who.

"Coffee and torture by socialite." She gave him a teasing grin. "You know, some girls might see that as a red flag."

"And what about this particular girl?" He looked at Julie with those quick intelligent eyes, a dimple forming next to the corner of his mouth.

Lord, it was a nice mouth.

"What good's a coffee without a little side discussion of murder?"

Julie's phone buzzed in her pocket, and she jolted. Miranda. Sassafras. "Sorry, as nice as caffeine with a side of murder sounds, I'm actually meeting with my thesis advisor." She glanced at her phone again. "Five minutes ago."

She rocked a step backwards. Already in retreat mode, wasn't she? The thought dampened her mood.

"Okay then." He gave a half smile, as though he could tell he was being let down easy. It made her think of the look on his face when the psychic had said something about a betrayal in his past. The quick comeback to cover the letdown. It struck a chord inside of Julie, who had also been burned too much by her past. She wanted to stamp that feeling out for both of them.

"Maybe another time?" she said, her voice gone shy and uncertain. Her stomach did a double flip. She held out her phone to him to program his number. His smile returned, less cocky, but no less brilliant.

"I'm Julie, by the way."

After returning her phone, he wrapped a strong hand around hers and shook.

"Griffin. Griffin Durocher."

All the cogs and wheels that made the world turn seemed to grind to a halt. Durocher. Just like Sophia Durocher, the subject of her thesis.

Julie had the odd sensation that everything—her detour to the psychic, her crash into Griffin, even her hand shaking his—was being orchestrated by some invisible puppet master's strings.

"What's the matter? You see one of the 'ghostly presences' this guy's always talking about?" Griffin tapped his copy of The Skeptics' Guide.

A nervous laugh escaped from Julie. Could this person with the full lips and penchant for obscure history really be Sophia's grandson? Should she just come out and ask? And even if he were, what did that mean? She opened her mouth to launch into the question, but wasn't sure she wanted to know the answer yet.

"Just thought of something related to my project."

CHAPTER 3

Later that afternoon, Julie stomped through her beloved courtyard, thoughts of Griffin Durocher and psychic predictions sidelined. The stairs leading to her apartment rattled under her angry footsteps.

Once inside, she navigated the obstacle course of wood planks and power tools and slammed her keys down on the kitchen counter. Then her books. Then her purse for good measure.

Suffice it to say, the meeting with her advisor had gone even worse than she'd hoped.

Are you certain you want to pursue this angle, Julie? Miranda had asked. I understand your ambition to prove yourself by uncovering something new, but Sophia took a plea bargain. She never contested the charges. I'd like you to consider another topic before you spend another year on an idea that will come to nothing.

Julie punched through the plastic sheeting hanging in the doorway to the master bedroom.

No, she didn't want to pick a new topic. Julie had blinked back the tears at the cafe, but swiped at the few that escaped now. How many months had she spent combing every police report and newspaper clipping, talking with Sophia's friends and neighbors, and studying everything about this case she could get her hands on? And now she had only two weeks before defending her final project proposal. Sophia was innocent. Julie might not be able to prove it yet, but she intended to find a way. If she couldn't get her own life in order, she at least wanted to help someone else. Even that was failing miserably.

Inside the master bedroom, Julie's blood pressure spiked even further. The behemoth of a bed her mom and dad had shared years before Julie had inherited the place stood mocking her from the center of the room, a stubborn monument to days—and disasters—gone by.

She frowned at its untouched sheets. It was the last thing Julie wanted a reminder of in her own space, but the bed was solid oak and refused to fit through the door frame, no matter how hard she'd tried.

Sidestepping the piles of still-unpacked boxes, Julie grabbed some yoga pants and hurried out to sulk and regroup.

She changed in the living room—the calm at the center of her storm—and switched on the TV to binge-watch some X-Files and drown her sorrows with homemade lemonade.

While the familiar theme song played, Julie grabbed some lemons, courtesy of her courtyard trees, and pulverized them as she surveyed the disaster that was her humble abode. Her apartment and the one next door that shared the courtyard had served as servants' quarters for a sprawling old home. It'd all been renovated around the turn of the century and could desperately use some further updates. Exposed wood peeked out from the edges of half-ripped-up carpet in the hall. Packs of tile and an array of drills and saws took up the better part of a bookshelf, like a curated exhibit of unused home improvement implements. This was not exactly what she thought being a homeowner would be like.

There were definitely plusses too, she supposed. The high-beamed kitchen and tiny balcony were just her style. And of course, her courtyard. Every time she walked its cobblestone path past rain gardens with a hundred jewel tones of green and lemon trees, it felt like her own secret garden. But even that wouldn't be just hers anymore if the moving trucks and footsteps on the other set of stairs over the past few days were any indication. There was only one other apartment here beyond the ironwork gates, and it had been vacant for as long as Julie could remember.

And then, of course, there was the master bedroom—filled to the ceiling beams with the ghosts of her parents' failed marriage. In her excitement at having the place to herself when her mom moved out a year ago, Julie had moved all of her things from the tiny back bedroom to the master, but it wasn't long before the wrongness of the room pressed in on her.

But she'd never really moved back to her old room. It felt like something she'd outgrown, and her mom's old room was something she didn't want to grow into. So she'd settled on the couch, caught somewhere in between.

Julie let the cool lemonade slide down her throat and tried to focus on Mulder and Scully to take her mind off her sour mood. Maybe their unorthodox methods would spark an idea that could jump-start her project again.

Just as her shoulders relaxed, her phone chimed. She plodded over to silence it for the duration of her pity party, but a text lit up the screen.

Hey, it's Griffin. Remember me?

The sight of his name gave Julie's heart a little jolt, but she shoved the phone back into her purse. No more curveballs from the universe tonight.

She flopped on her couch/bed but couldn't settle. Maybe it was 1997 TV, or maybe curiosity just got the best of her. Or maybe she had a craving for chaos after all.

She swiped to access the message.

I think we switched books.

Nerves trilled in her chest. She'd written all over that thing. Research notes, random free associations, and some stuff that was pretty personal.

Can we meet tonight to switch back? she typed furiously.

Sorry, can't tonight. I have a dinner thing with my family.

Julie paced, phone in hand. The vise squeezing her insides constricted further. If this kept up, her insides were going to look like they'd been through a blender.

Maybe he hadn't read any of it.

Rather enjoying your commentary, he texted.

You're reading my notes?! That's a violation of privacy.

Griffin replied, Sorry, couldn't help it. You've bewitched me with your words. This is like getting the Half-Blood Prince version of a potions book.

Let's just obliviate all that chicken scratch of mine you just read, mmkay?

Did you really get to see the diary entries from the LaLaurie's neighbor? he asked.

I thought I said obliviate.

I believe it's obliviATE.

Okay, so we've established I suck at spells.

But not at history, he replied. Good catch on the date mix up on the dueling oaks thing. I thought that sounded wrong.

I have a freakish memory for dates. But seriously, could you cease and desist with the reading of the margin notes, please? Some of that's personal.

Like your crush on that historian guy?

Excuse me?

I'll admit, he does have a big brain and knows a lot about pirates. But you've got to admit, I'm better looking, plus still alive. So I've got that going for me.

Julie smiled. Valid points.

Plus, I have insider knowledge about where to find the best chocolate pralines in the Quarter.

Can't pass up a chocolate praline.

Still want me to stop?

Julie stirred the ice cubes in her lemonade. Against all logic, she wasn't sure she did want him to stop.

He texted, You can read my notes if it makes you feel better. Even the stuff in the woo woo section.

By "woo woo" do you mean the ghostly stuff or the existential stuff?

The big mysteries of life. Why are we here? Why do we believe? Why has no one figured out how to make crème brûlée Oreos?

Someone needs to get on that, Julie answered.

Right? Anyway, it's not the sort of thing I usually share before a first date, but it's only fair since I've seen yours and all that.

I suppose it is only fair. I doubt your comments are as verbose and embarrassing as mine are.

You haven't opened the book yet, have you?

She rummaged through her purse until she found it and flipped through the pages. Instead of her looping introspective scrawl, neat block letters in various shades of blue crowded the margins. Coffee stains and doodles marked other pages. Question marks and intersecting lines. Julie ran a finger across his drawing of a stick figure sword fight. This felt more like an artifact, a conversation that stretched out across the years between writer and reader than a story between the covers.

We may have more in common than we originally thought, she wrote.

Listen, I've got to meet my brother, but speaking of first dates (see what I did there?), want to grab dinner later this week?

Julie bit her lip. That may depend on your reaction to the "woo woo" stuff. ;)

I like my odds. Mysteries of the universe first, dinner second. Why don't you do some reading and we'll make plans soon?

Good thing you don't lack any of Jean Lafitte's confidence.

Julie finished the conversation, grinning like an idiot.

So much for steering her own ship.

Touché, universe.

CHAPTER 4

But they didn't switch back the next day. Or the next day. Or the next.

Between their work schedules and research, they struggled to find a time to meet up. Or maybe Julie was stalling. Probably. She'd spent nearly as much time sifting through Griffin's thoughts in the margins of The Skeptics' Guide and exchanging flirty texts with him as she had doggedly pursued her research on Madame Sophia. Every exchange took her deeper into the inner workings of this kindred spirit who shared her taste in books and her intense unease with the unknown. His notes and his texts were by turns funny, intelligent, and poignant. She found her heart beating faster every time her phone lit up with an alert from this person who was almost certainly the grandson of Sophia Durocher.

Julie smirked at his latest text and flipped open his copy of The Skeptics' Guide on her bathroom counter as she got ready for work. A doodle of Pac-Man-style ghosts filled in with green and orange highlighter filled the margins of the next page. Above one ghost, he'd drawn a speech bubble with an arrow pointing to a nearby passage.

Reminds me of that Nietzsche quote I had to memorize in PHI 101.

Word, read the other ghost's speech bubble. "With the unknown, one is confronted with danger, discomfort, and care; the first instinct is to abolish these painful states."

The sentiment sent a reverberation through Julie's chest.

She typed, At least I'm not going around spouting Nietzsche. :)

Too pretentious? In my defense, I didn't know anyone else would ever read these notes.

I think Inky and Blinky toned it down. Kind of serious in the front, party in the back. Like the mullet of margin notes.

If I ever publish my commentary I'm stealing that for a cover quote.

Julie smiled to herself and pulled on the fluffy Victorian skirt that served as her work uniform. She caught sight of her goofy grin in the mirror.

Oh boy, this was a bad idea, wasn't it?

Julie texted, Gotta go. Leaving for work in a few.

You ever going to tell me where this mysterious work is?

Weren't you just saying something about mystery and allure?

Fine, don't tell me. I've got a project I'm working on tonight too. Two actually.

What sort of projects?, she asked.

The first involves packing.

Moving? Julie's disappointment at the prospect startled her.

Just across town, he replied. Inherited a place from some distant relatives. It's been sitting empty for the last ten years. A fixer-upper.

Julie: My apartment's an old family place too. I've been trying to rehab it since my mom moved out, but other projects keep getting in the way. Speaking of projects, what's the second one?

It involves ghosts and busting.

You're making popcorn and watching that Bill Murray movie from the 80s?

Yep.

Really?

Nope. Something a little more active than that.

Julie pulled on her low-cut but still decent for work top to complete her ensemble. Should I send holy water?

:) I'll let you know.

Meet up with me later?

Julie bit her lip and thought back to Griffin's quote about wanting to stamp out the swirl of feelings that came with the unknown. Danger—check. Discomfort—check. Care—as much as she didn't like to admit it—check. The urge to abolish all three painful states like a mofo was strong at the moment. But equally strong was the surge of warmth and irrepressible desire to see where all of this heated history-inspired flirting might lead.

Julie texted back, I'll let you know. :)

CHAPTER 5

Humming to herself, Julie stepped into Deveauxs' Historical Haunts: Tours and Gifts. It wasn't unusual for her to be in a good mood when she got to work, but this felt a little ridiculous, even for her.

The familiar smells of bergamot and cedar filled her senses. She spotted her cousin Wendy's mass of red curls at the back of the shop and weaved through tourists perusing the masks, good luck charms, and souvenir gris-gris bags. Though Julie's hair fell in sepia-toned waves, it always gave Julie a surge of pride when someone asked if they were sisters. They had the same smart mouths, penchants for tall boots, and insolent curves to their hips. En route to her cousin, she tried to tone down her enthusiasm, lest she never hear the end of it.

But as soon as Julie approached the checkout counter, her uncle Rob's fist slammed down near the computer. Mini-Voodoo dolls and plastic shot glasses attached to Mardi Gras throws went toppling. Julie rescued a stack of bookmarks before they hit the floor.

Several tourists looked up, alarm and confusion in their shared glances.

"Don't mind him," Wendy said in her stage voice. "Dad's really into creating the ghostly ambiance."

"What's got him in such a tizzy?" Julie whispered when she reached her cousin.

"That guy from the DEBUNKED website. You know, the one who goes to all the paranormal attractions and tries to say they're bullshit."

"Ah."

Her usually calm uncle stormed back to his office and let out a barely stifled roar.

"He did a post about the vampire tour and we've had twenty-three cancellations already today."

Julie's gaze flitted to Uncle Rob's office again. As he stared at the computer screen, his face grew redder.

She grabbed an ectoplasm stress ball from the display and tossed it over the counter onto his desk. He grunted, and his face went from scarlet to a less angry shade of pink at the sight of his niece.

"Do I need to get you one of those cat posters with an uplifting slogan?" Julie strode into the office and planted a kiss on her uncle's forehead.

"What you can get me is a poster of this DEBUNKED guy so I can throw darts at his head." Rob harrumphed and guzzled straight from his bottle of Maalox.

Julie eyed the worry lines creasing her uncle's face.

"I'll be fine," Rob said. "Did you get the tile saw I left for you? I can help you do the cuts this weekend."

"Thanks. This'll all blow over before you know it."

Rob grunted again.

"Ooh, look at Mr. Hottie over there checking you out." Once Julie had returned to the gift shop, Wendy nudged her and nodded toward a perfectly attractive guy in jeans and a logo t-shirt by the zombie arcade games.

He smiled at Julie and took in the high slit in her skirt with an appreciative sweep of his gaze.

Julie gave him a once-over. Hot in a vaguely superhero movie guy sort of way. Flirty eye contact. Double fisting Hurricanes from next door, which screamed tourist. Casual fun she could easily walk away from. Normally this would've been Julie catnip.

Tonight, it lacked the usual appeal.

Julie shrugged and let her eyes roam the rest of the gathering crowd.

"You're really hung up on this book guy, aren't you?" Wendy said. "Maybe he's your book soulmate."

Julie snorted. "He cannot be my book soulmate because soulmates are like the tooth fairy."

"Loaded and likely to pay you nighttime visits?"

"No." Julie laughed. "Something you believe in until you have enough sense not to."

"Your 'book familiar' then." Wendy gave her a playful jab. After a time check, she called out for eight o'clock tour participants. She and Julie stepped out of the store and onto the street.

"Voodoo tour, please line up behind this sign here, " Wendy announced. "Ghost tour over there."

Julie turned and stopped in her tracks. Ten feet away, Griffin leaned against a streetlamp, reading a brochure. The shadowy light accentuated the lines of his jaw.

Her heart jumped into her throat. It was weird that he knew her deepest thoughts about the afterlife, but not where she worked or how she took her coffee. She wasn't prepared for this.

"He's here," Julie hissed to Wendy.

"Who's here?"

"The tooth fairy. He's got a tour ticket." She nodded in Griffin's direction.

Wendy's gaze locked onto him and went from curious to flinty in a split second.

"Oh, no, he didn't come back here." Wendy launched herself toward Griffin at an intimidating gait.

"Wen?" Julie called, trying to keep up. Wendy halted inches from Griffin's face.

"You." She poked him in the chest and flung the word at him like it was laced with arsenic.

Griffin straightened, stunned, gaze moving from Wendy to Julie and back again.

"Wendy, what are you doing?" Julie pulled her cousin's shoulder and angled her away from Griffin. Wendy seethed.

"Hey, Julie." Griffin said, his voice cautious. He stepped away from Wendy and took in Julie's costume and name tag. His brows creased. "You're a ghost tour operator?"

Wendy didn't give her a chance to answer. "How dare you come back here after all the damage you've already caused my family with your little article? Do you know how many bookings we've lost because of your stupid website?"

Julie's heart tanked. Griffin was the DEBUNKED guy?

"That was you?" Julie said.

His frown was conflicted. "I wrote a post about your vampire tour, yes."

"Your new friend here gets his kicks by destroying people's businesses," Wendy said.

A muscle in Griffin's jaw ticked. "No, I get my kicks by exposing the truth, letting people know what they're getting into so they don't get swindled and lied to."

"Well, you can go 'expose the truth' somewhere else and shove it up your ass," Wendy said.

Griffin squared his stance. "I'm afraid I've already bought my ticket." He waved the printout in his hand.

"Well, I'll happily give you a refund." Wendy snatched his ticket. "All in pennies."

She huffed off and disappeared through the crowd, leaving Julie and Griffin alone.

"Not exactly the way I imagined our second meeting going." Griffin blew out a breath and raked a hand through his hair. "Your friend is... intense."

"She's my cousin. And she's protective." Her words had turned sharp. "My uncle's been having a coronary since that article went up. He would not take kindly to seeing you out here."

"If you're sticking to the truth and not blowing smoke up people's asses, you've got nothing to worry about."

Julie's blood neared its boiling point. Her family's tour company was the best and most historically accurate place around. Uncle Rob, Wendy, and Julie had worked their asses off to earn that reputation. They consistently had five-star reviews on TripAdvisor, and the Travel Channel had even done a profile on them. Plus, Deveauxs' prided itself on being the company most beloved of the locals, who had stronger bullshit detectors than the tourists. It wasn't like the vampire tour promised actual vampires, just local lore, vampire lifestyle, and Anne Rice stuff. There was no way there was anything less than aboveboard, unless...

Julie's stomach curdled. "Let me guess, you had Norman as your tour guide, didn't you? He embellishes a bit."

Griffin laughed. "I believe his exact words were, 'And then the vampire chased me under the streetlight, and I swear, she started to sparkle.'"

Julie groaned. "Yeah, well, he does have a flair for the dramatic." He also had a stern warning from Uncle Rob not to play to the Twilight fangirls anymore.

"Maybe your uncle should stick to the competent tour guides, and we'd all be on the same side."

His tone wasn't malicious, but Julie's hackles rose all the same. "Maybe if you'd stick to not insulting my family, we'd all be on the same side."

Griffin's cocky expression fled, his hangdog face making him look suitably contrite. "I'm sorry. That came out wrong. I just meant that I'd rather have a tour guide like you who obviously knows her history. And the difference between fact and fiction."

The fire in Julie's temper cooled a bit.

"Truce?" Hope played in his green eyes behind his glasses.

She folded her arms over her chest and tried to sort through the conflicting onslaught of emotions his gaze stirred up. She needed more time to sort this out. "Maybe. A conditional truce."

"I'll take it."

She jabbed his chest. "But you say one ill word about my family business again, and that truce is over."

"Deal." Griffin moved closer. "So, what's on our agenda for the ghost tour tonight? Haunted hotels? The LaLaurie mansion? Tales of poison and murder?"

Julie spotted Wendy's flame-colored hair bobbing through the crowd, and anxiety sizzled through her veins. "I don't think you sticking around for the tour is such a good idea. My uncle has one of Jean Lafitte's swords, and he's not afraid to use it."

"What's the first stop, then? I'll catch up later incognito."

Julie hesitated. "I don't know..."

Griffin spun around. "Let's see. From here, you could probably start at Pirate's Alley. Or maybe Bottom of the Cup to visit your namesake. Or..." He faced the other direction, and Julie tried not to give anything away. "It is close to Halloween, so Yo Mama's is probably on the agenda."

Julie stiffened and felt her ears go red. It was like her body was incapable of keeping pertinent information to itself. Griffin's smile widened just before Wendy heaved a bag full of pennies at Griffin's feet.

"Here's your refund, dickhead. Now get lost. Jules, why are you still talking to this guy?"

"He's just leaving. Aren't you?" Julie asked.

Griffin flashed Wendy a rather friendly smile, especially considering the girl might've just broken both of his big toes with coin rolls—Julie had to give him points for that—and nodded. "Sorry to cause any trouble."

Wendy grumbled all the way back to her tour group.

Griffin leaned close to Julie's ear. Not here. Not here. Not here. Julie's pulse raced as he grazed her skin.

"See you at Yo Mama's," he whispered.

CHAPTER 6

Julie didn't miss a beat, leading her tour down St. Peter past the boisterous crowd spilling out of Pat O'Brien's, even though her head was a jumble of discordant thoughts. If Griffin showed up down the street, she should really turn him away. On top of the fact that he'd pissed off her uncle, there was the matter of all tours leading to Sophia Durocher's house. Who knew what that would be like for him, hearing his grandmother's alleged murders rehashed? But surely, if he did his research the way she thought he did, he knew that was coming and had shown up, anyway.

She sighed. The memory of his breath on her skin lingered and ignited her senses. But this had just gotten a whole lot more complicated. She couldn't reconcile the Griffin who sent funny texts and musings about history with the Griffin who trounced their family business. The guy she'd gotten to know over the last week was skeptical, sure, but not mean-spirited. There had to be some misunderstanding. Until Julie smoothed it out, though, it was probably wise for Griffin to keep his distance.

At the same time, though, Julie's pride was a fierce thing, and it would hardly abide Griffin walking away thinking Deveauxs' was just another mediocre tourist trap.

Julie herded tonight's tour group past Preservation Hall and came to a stop in front of the green shutters of Yo Mama's. The long vertical windows stood open. Gauzy curtains billowed out, along with the smell of hamburgers and fries from the restaurant. No sign of Griffin. Even so, her senses were on alert for his presence.

A sense of exhilaration and rightness that accompanied doing what she loved best came over Julie as she launched into her official tour spiel. As always, she started with her credentials as a lifetime NOLA resident and lover of all things historical, and then mentioned the master's degree she was pursuing in Folklore and Pop Culture—yes, this was actually a thing—at New Orleans City College.

She'd lost herself in the rhythm of the tour when the front door of the former tailor shop swung open. Griffin sauntered out, beer in hand, and lounged against the wall. Julie was used to distractions, and though she hid it well, his presence stirred a warmth in her.

"As I was saying—" Julie started.

"What's the story with all the masks around here?" a tourist with a Midwestern accent broke in.

"They're an important part of Mardi Gras culture," Julie said. "Wearing the masks was a way for people to be free, to have a bit of fun without being chained to who they were supposed to be and how their family and social class dictated they act. During that one night of revelry, at least."

It felt like that's what she and Griffin had been doing, enjoying whatever this flirtation was in anonymity. But now that the masks had come off and reality had set in, what happened next?

Griffin flashed her that infuriatingly gorgeous grin and sipped his beer. "Did you know that the people on Mardi Gras parade floats are required by law—"

"To wear masks? Yes." Julie crossed her arms over her chest.

Griffin's eyes glinted in the streetlight. She had to send him on his way or set up some boundaries, stat.

"Oh hey, is that Nicolas Cage?" She pointed to the street.

Her guests turned to check for themselves.

She stepped closer to Griffin. He tilted his chin down, and when he met her gaze, a wave of heat crackled between them. "As much as I enjoy your guest-hosting skills and want to give you an accurate idea of the quality of our tours, I don't have a good feeling about this."

Griffin gave her a mock-pout, and Julie shook her head.

"I'm serious. If you're going to come along, you're going to have to behave."

"Define behave." His gaze dipped to her lips.

Julie tried to ignore the way heat pooled in her core at the heady combination of Griffin in proximity and the suggestion of misbehavior. She swatted at his chest. "I mean it. First, this is not for public record. No more negative publicity about my family business on that blog of yours."

Griffin nodded.

"Promise," she prompted.

"I promise, not a negative word on the blog about Deveauxs' Historical Haunts."

Her shoulders relaxed. "And any sign of my cousin, you make yourself scarce. She'll cool down in a few days, but let me handle her."

"I think I can work with that."

Her final concern popping up, Julie bit her lip. "You know the itinerary of the tour, right? Most of the popular stops we make?" She didn't want to come out and say it. *We're going to your grandmother's house. To talk about the murders she allegedly committed. Can you handle that?*

An unreadable expression crossed his features, and Julie second-guessed her judgment, but his cocky smile quickly made a reappearance.

"Yeah, I know what I'm getting into."

Julie's stomach flipped, and she felt suddenly unmoored. Did she know what she was getting into? Unquestionably, categorically, not.

But with her most pressing concerns assuaged and tourists regrouped, she did what she did best—carried on.

"Who wants to hear about the tailor who accidentally hanged himself while he was trying to create the ultimate Halloween display?"

CHAPTER 7

"You guys should be a permanent tour guide team," a girl in goth makeup and a Pokemon sweater said a few stops later. Julie and Griffin had just finished a spirited debate at Bottom of the Cup tea shop about the legend of the mischievous ghost who shared Julie's name. Although his intrusion into her tour routine had chafed at first, she was beginning not to mind so much. Several others in the group voiced their assent.

Griffin shot Julie a rakish grin. She rolled her eyes, but couldn't help the easy smile that slid onto her face. They'd hit Pirate's Alley, the singing rain, and the Mississippi River Bottom, playing off of each other at each stop. There wasn't much she didn't know about the ghosts and legends that haunted the Quarter, but he'd surprised her more than once.

"Sorry guys, this is a one night kind of thing," she said.

She had to admit, even though he was messing with her usual flow, the chance to match wits with someone just as passionate as she was about her city's history was exhilarating. Sure, she could geek out about it with Wendy, but Wendy didn't exactly concern herself with ghosts in her free time. Griffin, on the other hand, might have an internet search history as weird as her own.

And then there was the way he examined everything. He challenged some things she took on faith and had believed for so long she'd forgotten to turn a critical eye on them. No one ever did that with her—not that she'd let anyone get close enough to try.

En route to the Provincial Hotel, Julie looked up just in time to see Wendy's tour heading their way. Though her cousin walked backwards, she expertly navigated the potholes and puddles, but at any second she could turn around and not like what she saw.

Crap. Julie should've been paying more attention.

Grabbing Griffin by the shoulders, she steered him down the nearest street. "This way, everybody. A little detour on the way to the LaLaurie mansion."

Once they were safely down the street and out of Wendy's sight, Julie slowed and looked back at the group.

Griffin hung back, eyes stony, and hands thrust in his pockets. Was he really pissed that Julie had tried to hide him from her cousin?

Then Julie looked up at the grey-painted brickwork and the ornate door of the Sophia Durocher house, and her stomach and throat seemed to switch places.

If she hadn't been so distracted by this verbal sparring with Griffin, maybe she would've mentally prepared for this tour stop. She'd never explicitly asked about his relationship with Sophia, though she had her suspicions. He said he was okay with coming here, but the truth of it was there in the way he regarded the house with a mixture of familiarity and loathing. He met her gaze, and his Adam's apple bobbed.

Frantically searching for a way to stop the hurt in his eyes, Julie blurted, "We can skip this one tonight."

"What do you mean skip the Durocher house?" a couple from Iowa groused. "It's a week before Halloween. That's the whole reason we came on this tour."

More exasperated voices chimed in.

Sassafras. If she skipped the main attraction, all these people would complain. Complaining would lead to questions from Uncle Rob and even more lost bookings chalked up to a certain blogger.

But one look at Griffin's face, now devoid of all of playful swagger, made her hesitate.

Griffin's gaze moved from Julie to the now churlish crowd scrolling through their distraction of choice on their phones. How quickly they turned.

Griffin shook his head, but his expression remained as shuttered as his grandmother's house. "It's fine. Just—" He flipped a hand at the house and strode back to the edge of the group.

Julie's stomach gave a sick pang at the thought of rubbing lemon juice into Griffin's old wounds. But she also had a duty to her uncle, especially after all he'd done for her over the years.

After a steadying breath, Julie soldiered over to the ironwork door under the upper gallery.

"Fifteen years ago — technically fifteen years ago next week, on Halloween—two of the most puzzling and grisly murders in recent New Orleans history occurred right in this very house."

An excited murmur rippled through the crowd. Phones slid out of sight, and attention returned to Julie. Her shoulders slumped in relief. She had them again.

Griffin, not so much.

"This place was once home and workplace to mild-mannered, friendly neighborhood psychic, Madame Sophia Durocher. Who, by the way, was also the proprietress of the neighborhood soup kitchen. By all accounts, Sophia wouldn't hurt a fly, but on the night of October 31, 2001, two less-than-savory clients entered and never came out alive. Forty stab wounds each. And they found Sophia holding the bloody knife."

A couple of girls in the back stood on tiptoes, angling for a peek inside.

"Here's the official story of what happened that night, but I'm not the only one who thinks there might've been other forces at work."

At this, Griffin tilted his head and regarded Julie with cautious interest.

"That night, Santero and Ackerman, a couple of dirty politicians who were also ringleaders of a prostitution ring, arrived for their appointment with Sophia at six-thirty. The place was empty except for one other client, Marie Reynard, who had mistakenly arrived an hour early for her reading and was waiting in the parlor. She and Sophia had tea before the gentlemen's arrival.

"According to Marie's testimony, she heard arguing coming from the parlor. The men made threats against Sophia. Something about blackmail. When the screaming began, Marie raced into the parlor to see if Sophia needed help, but Sophia appeared perfectly capable of helping herself.

"Marie described feeling a coldness overtake her when she stepped through the parlor door, something she'd always associated with spirits, something that chilled her to the marrow.

"Marie found both men splayed out on the floor. Sophia knelt over them, plunging the knife into their flesh over and over again."

Julie continued with Marie's account of Sophia appearing possessed. The group leaned closer in rapt attention, but there was not so much as a peep from Griffin. Not that she could blame him.

Every time she caught sight of Griffin's guarded green eyes, she felt more like a horrible person. Only years of practice and the intimate knowledge of the Sophia Durocher case enabled her to push through.

"And so Sophia came to, covered in blood with no memory of the previous hours."

"So you're saying she was possessed?" a tourist asked.

Griffin's jaw ticked.

"Some people think so. Or just really, really against prostitution." Julie wanted to snatch the words back as soon as they'd left her mouth. Why did her mind always go for humor when nerves hit, even when wildly inappropriate?

"And what do you think?" the Pokemon Goth asked.

"Self-defense?" offered another tourist.

Julie considered how to put it. It was a gut feeling more than anything. Years of telling the story and holding it up to the light to see different angles. Despite evidence and testimony to the contrary, especially now that Julie had talked to her friends and neighbors, she couldn't see a way that this woman who baked muffins for the hungry and took in strays was a murderer.

Griffin stayed in his fortress of solitude pose, but he shifted slightly. Something in the way his whole body braced told her that whatever she was about to say mattered to him.

Julie took a deep breath. "I don't think you stab someone forty times in self-defense. Something like that is personal. Yet there's nothing to suggest Sophia ever met those two before that night."

"But what about the note and the hush money?" a girl from the group asked.

That's what had ultimately damned Sophia, and the one thing that had never tracked for Julie. Before they found the note asking for Sophia's silence about their prostitution ring and the cash for her pains, there was no motive for the murders. After it surfaced, though, the case was practically closed before it began. The lawyers had strongly advised Sophia to take the plea bargain rather than drag her family through the agony of a long, drawn-out, very public case that would ultimately end in prison time, anyway.

"Yeah, but why write a note and leave evidence of criminal activity? If they were going to see her, why not just tell her in person they wanted to pay her to keep her mouth shut?"

"But no one else was there," the dude from Iowa said.

"According to Marie Reynard, maybe." Julie chanced a glance at Griffin again. His chin tilted upward, his expression now pensive rather than closed off. Julie loosed a breath. It was a start.

"But Marie disappeared the next day, and nobody ever heard from her again. What if she was lying? Or what if she was threatened by the actual killer and skipped town? Or maybe she was the killer herself."

By the time they reached the LaLaurie Mansion, a sad weight had settled in Julie's stomach.

Griffin hadn't ditched the tour, but he'd walked in near silence the whole way there, hands stuffed in his pockets. Griffin met all her discreet attempts to apologize with one or two-word answers.

He lingered at the back of the crowd, and something twisted inside of her. It seemed she'd be flying solo once again.

That was okay, though. She was used to it. Good at it, even. Maybe this was a sign that she should walk away now, before she got in too deep. Before her inevitable retreat.

But everything jumbled inside of her. After tonight and the past few days of exchanging texts and reading each other's musings, and all of tonight's flirtations, her inner GPS had shifted. An exit strategy wasn't foremost on her mind.

Unfortunately, Griffin seemed to be the one moving away.

Julie plastered on a smile and went into autopilot on the story of socialite murderess Delphine LaLaurie. Just when she'd resigned herself to going back to being her usual one-woman tour guide extraordinaire, she felt Griffin's tall form beside her.

She looked up to see a half-smile had returned to his face. He pushed up his glasses, and when he spoke, it was a white flag and a gift.

"You want to tell them about the 'ghosts' in the hidden room, or should I?"

CHAPTER 8

"What do you say we grab some drinks, have our first date a day early?" Griffin asked.

The tour had finished up, and most of the group was now shouting cocktail orders over the loud music or taking pictures of the fireplace in Lafitte's Blacksmith Shop.

"Tell you what," Julie said. "Why don't I give you a private tour of an establishment that's not on the usual circuit anymore?"

Across town, just outside of the touristy part of the Quarter, Miss Peacock's teemed with people knocking back drinks called things like The Red Herring and The Rook and The Bishop (that one was only slid across the bar diagonally), while engaged in boisterous board games.

"A board game-themed bar? I like this place already," Griffin said.

"It's one of my favorite places. The owner's a friend of my mom's." Julie gestured to the framed photos of a blonde woman with Tim Curry and Robin Williams amid the game boards and pieces plastered to the walls.

After the upheaval of the last few hours, Julie practically melted into the comfort of the scarlet chair at the end of the bar. Griffin slid in next to her and scooted closer until their thighs nearly touched. The closeness and casual confidence of the gesture felt so right it sent warmth singing through her veins. At least for a few hours. Maybe she could be just a girl talking to a cute boy, not a ghost tour operator having some ill-advised fun with her family business's mortal enemy.

"You're a natural out there," Griffin said.

Julie flushed and took a sip of her rum and Coke.

"Thanks. You're not so bad yourself. If you ever wanted to trade in the myth busting and blogging for historical tour guiding, you'd be awesome at it."

"Somehow I don't think your uncle would be clamoring to hire me." He shot her a grin. "How long have you been doing this, anyway?"

"Tour guiding or collecting historical facts?"

He took a swig of his beer. "Both."

"Birth?" She smiled. "When I was little, my mom read me a book about a civilization that existed before written history. And they had these chosen people, the Storykeepers, whose job was to keep all the stories for the future generations. They memorized the history and the legends of their people and were basically like living libraries. They always fascinated me. I wanted to be one when I grew up. So when other girls were playing My Little Ponies, I was memorizing encyclopedias and acting out the Spanish conquest of New Orleans."

A sudden wave of shyness fluttered in her chest. She rarely shared all of this.

"And I've been tour guiding since I was seventeen and finally wore my uncle down," she added, not sure what else to say next.

She glanced up at Griffin through her lashes, and he gazed back at her, a thoughtful look on his chiseled features.

"I used to pretend my GI Joes were privateers. I carved them muskets out of twigs from my backyard."

Julie's shyness dissipated at the sight of his crooked grin. Lord, he had a gorgeous smile. The usual one with its easy confidence was nice too, but this one felt like a peek at a different side of him, a more vulnerable one.

The back door opened, sending in a surge of humid air. Julie gathered up her hair and pressed her glass to her neck to cool down. Condensation slid down her neck, bringing blessed relief. Even though it was nearly the end of October, the weather was unseasonably hot and humid.

She turned to see Griffin watching her with something primal in his eyes. She felt that look, dizzying and white-hot, all over her skin. The sensation heated her to the core and sent her imagination into overdrive picturing what she'd like to do if they were some place more private.

It took her a moment to recover her powers of speech.

"You said before that you were doing grad work too. What are you studying?" she asked.

"History and Construction Management."

"Interesting combination."

"I like historical projects. And I took so many history courses I figured I might as well get another degree out of it."

They talked some more over a game of Battleship before they circled back to the ghostly stuff.

"Okay, so tell the truth. You don't really believe in all of that ghostly stuff, do you?" His eyes dancing, Griffin leaned back in his mustard-colored chair.

"I guess you could say I don't not believe."

"Okay. I don't not understand what you're saying." Dimples punctuated his smile, and his eyes crinkled at the corners.

She swatted at him. "I've experienced some very weird stuff in my ghost touring days."

"Is that a technical term?"

"It is, actually. Very Weird Stuff, TM."

The fabric of his jeans grazed the bare flesh of her leg, making it suddenly hard to concentrate.

"Such as?" he prompted.

"Cold spots in rooms. Walking into places and feeling all the hair on my arms stand on end. I can't definitively say what I felt was ghostly. But I'm not 100% sure it wasn't, either. I like to allow for the existence of things I can't explain."

Griffin nodded sagely. "Like Justin Bieber."

"Exactly. Or selfie sticks."

They grinned at each other. The way those piercing green eyes of his roved over her face brought on a sumptuous wave of heat that would put a NOLA summer to shame.

The bartender slid two orange-colored shots their way. "Two Revolvers. Compliments of our lovely proprietress, Gina. She said she'd come say hi in a bit."

Griffin clinked his glass against Julie's, and they tossed them back.

"Why are you so convinced that there's no such thing as ghosts?" Julie took a sip of her other drink to chase the burn of the shot.

He stretched back in his chair with a gleam in his eyes. Julie couldn't help admiring the long planes of his chest.

"Because I'm a rational human."

"So am I," she shot back. "But how can you say something doesn't exist just because you haven't witnessed it?"

"I reserve the right to change my mind. You got any proof I should see?"

"Maybe." Julie's gaze moved to the staircase, and her lips curved up in a secret smile.

When the owner came by to visit, Julie asked, "Hey, Gina, you mind if I show my friend here the billiard room and see if Charlie's out and about tonight?"

Gina tossed her a set of keys. "I've got it closed for renovations, but you can check it out."

Julie motioned for Griffin to follow her. He swung a leg over the chain blocking access to the narrow stairwell and followed Julie up.

"So I take it Charlie is the resident ghost of this place?"

"Mmm hmm. I'm not making any promises about sightings, but I have felt some pretty otherworldly things in this room before."

"Otherworldly, huh?"

Julie paused at the top of the stairs, and Griffin's momentum knocked him into her, setting her off balance. His breath tickled her ear, and his scent pressed into her—sweat mingled with cologne that made her think of a pine forest. Griffin caught her arm and steadied her. The contact of his palm was delicious on her skin. His strong fingers skimmed down her arm until they rested on the small of her back. The whole thing conspired with the shot to envelop her in a warm, off-balanced feeling.

"So this trouble-making blog of yours, what's the story there?" Julie asked, trying to recover.

Their footsteps echoed on the wooden floorboards, and the sound of the music and crowd faded as they went down the hallway. There was something thrilling about having the whole second floor to themselves.

"Just something I started a few years ago."

"To suck the joy out of tourist attractions?" She shot him a saucy look.

"No. Tourist attractions are fine. What I have a problem with is people getting duped by people they put their trust in—psychics, tour operators. So I test things out and report back when places are just blowing smoke up people's asses."

"Like our vampire tour."

At the door marked Billiard Room, Julie jangled the keys into the lock.

"Look, I'm sorry about that. Truly. But that Norman guy was talking about glittery vegan vampires. What was I supposed to think?"

Julie sighed.

"Think you can forgive me?" Griffin asked. "I have a much higher opinion of Deveauxs' after tonight."

Julie shot him a teasing grin and shrugged. "I'm here, aren't I?"

Door now open, she fumbled until dim fluorescents illuminated the cozy room's worn leather couches and congregations of mismatched barstools. Green felt gleamed from the pool table in the center of the room.

"Think you can keep an open mind about the possibility of unknown entities up here?"

"I'm here, aren't I?" After a crooked grin, he leaned closer so that his lips grazed her ear. "Though I have to confess, the prospect of exploring this old building with you is more appealing than hanging out with ghosts."

The heat of his breath sent ripples of pleasure reverberating all over. He swept her hair to the side and pressed his lips to her neck.

"Sweet St. Expedite," she murmured.

"In need of an expedient solution, huh?" Griffin's teeth grazed her earlobe, and Julie's breath hitched.

"Might be."

"Did you know"—he trailed slow, lingering kisses along her neck and the line of her jaw until she thought she might go mad with desire—"that our old patron saint is also the patron saint of nerds?"

"Even better. Did you know"—Julie spun until their bodies aligned and she tasted the salt of his skin up the hollow of his throat—"that the people at Our Lady of Guadalupe thought that was his name because it said expedite on the shipment of saint statues?"

Unable to quell the heat that rushed her senses, Julie crushed her lips to his. The sweet taste of his cinnamon gum played through her senses as she threaded her fingers through his hair. His muscular arms pulled her close.

When he pulled back, he gazed at her, eyes heavy-lidded. "I really like you, Julie Deveaux."

He planted a kiss on her nose, and that unguarded smile graced his face. Something new and unfamiliar blossomed inside of her at the words. Their chests heaved against one another, both of them still breathless.

"I..." Julie hesitated, feeling like she was walking across a high-wire with no net below. "I like you too."

He pulled her to him and stroked her hair as she rested her head on his chest. She reveled in the sensation of having someone to lean on, though it also unsettled her.

"But as much as I would like to continue with our activities, you're not getting off that easy, my skeptical friend." Arching an eyebrow at him, she strode to the door, closed it, and turned the lock. "What do you say, ghost hunting first...exploring later."

Griffin's gaze, with its mix of reverence and desire, was a thief that stole her breath away.

"Exploring later. I can work with that." He laced his fingers with hers. "Okay, so, how do we do this?"

"Charlie?" Julie strode into the center of the room, trying to cool her senses and give herself a chance to think. "You here tonight?"

Griffin followed. "No answer. Rude."

"Hey, maybe ghosts are subtle. Also, no vocal cords." Julie started toward the left side of the room, where the mirror covered the top third of the wall. "I guess we walk around the room, feel for cold spots?"

Griffin veered right, pausing and looking up at regular intervals. She raised an eyebrow at him.

"I hear air-conditioning vents also cause those." He pointed up and kept walking. "So, you've actually felt the cold spots in here?"

"Yeah. It was very weird."

"What's this Charlie guy's story, anyway?"

"Pretty tragic. They say sometimes souls of addicts linger on even after they've left this plane. Hence so many stories of bar hauntings."

"I'm definitely not hanging around a bar for all eternity when I go. A library, maybe."

Julie smiled. "Feel anything?"

"I definitely feel something."

Her skin heated. "Anything cold?"

"Nope. You?"

"No." Julie walked in front of the pool table until a chill hit her and goosebumps coated her skin. "Wait. Got something. Come here."

He approached, halting only inches from her.

"Do you feel it?"

He canted his head to the side, considering. "Not really."

Julie's eyes widened as the chill wrapped around her shoulders and nipped at her nose. A wild sensation of having something out of her ken happening enveloped her.

"Come here," she said, teeth chattering.

Griffin closed the distance between them.

"Now do you feel it?" she asked.

A wrinkle formed between Griffin's brows. "I don't know. A little cold, maybe. What's it supposed to feel like?"

"Like icicles on your skin. The way the world holds its breath before the snow."

She held up her arm. Griffin skimmed a hand over the raised gooseflesh on her forearm.

His eyes widened, then flashed to the ceiling.

"No vent anywhere nearby," she said. "Already checked. Here, maybe you're not close enough."

When he took her place, a sense of wonder filled his face, like he was a kid who'd just seen his first magic trick.

"Now, do you believe me?" Julie crossed her arms in satisfaction.

"The air feels sort of dense, too," he said.

"Right?" The giddiness of discovery was contagious.

Griffin spun in circles and rubbed his forearms. "Maybe it's some kind of temperature sweet spot created by the ventilation system. Like the audio one in the Capitol Building in D.C. where you stand in the right spot and you can hear conversations from across the room."

Julie laughed and eased herself up onto the edge of the pool table. The ruffles of her skirt parted at the slit. "Or maybe it's one of those things that logic or rational means can 't explain."

"I'm still holding out for logic." His eyes sparkled. "But yeah, maybe."

Julie pulled him until he stood before her. "Crazy things happen all the time."

"Like meeting you." He tucked a strand of hair behind Julie's ear. "Of all the girls in all the world, I collide with the one who happens to be reading the same arcane book as I am. And it just so happens, that girl also laughs at my jokes and could quite possibly mop the floor with me in a NOLA trivia challenge."

"Quite possibly." Grinning, she leaned into the hand that rested on her cheek and let her eyes fall closed with the heady feeling of being here with him.

When she opened them again, she watched his gaze sweep over her.

"God, you're gorgeous." The words, in that low husky voice, made her feel bare somehow. She hooked her fingers into his belt loops and drew him to her. She widened her thighs until the planes of his torso pressed against her chest, like that could shield her from the vulnerable sensation.

"You forgot funny," she said. Laughter shook his chest against hers.

"I didn't forget. I just haven't gotten to that part yet."

"Good." The moment she met his gaze, her pulse galloped. He pushed up his glasses, and the light played on the lines of his jaw. He was a wonder and a discovery in and of himself. She didn't think she'd ever tire of looking at his face or hearing his voice. The guy who quoted dead philosophers and joked with her about historical duels. The guy who had access to her innermost thoughts and still stood here, looking at her like that.

Lust, she was well acquainted with, but it was the unabashed affection in his green eyes that undid her. She felt laid bare all over again.

At the same instant, they moved toward each other, hands reaching, lips moving, skin and salt and an unbearable need to be nearer, two pieces of star stuff pulled into each other's orbit.

This was not casual. Not playing by her hard and fast rules of moving along before she got hurt. But she could no more tear herself away than stop from drawing breath.

Julie held fast to Griffin's waist and shifted her weight. The resulting friction sent a delicious wave of longing through her.

Griffin's answering moan reverberated through every cell and electrified her body.

"Does this conclude the ghost hunting portion of the evening?" Griffin asked, breathless.

"I vote yes." Julie kissed the spot below his ear, eliciting another low groan.

"Any ideas how you'd like to spend the rest of the evening?"

Julie wrapped her legs around him and leaned up to whisper some choice suggestions in his ear.

Griffin gripped her hips and melted against her. "I knew I liked the way your mind worked."

Julie let out a breathy laugh.

"And Charlie, if you're still hanging around, get lost. We're going to need some privacy."

CHAPTER 9

The next afternoon, Julie sifted through her mail, humming a tune while she waited for Wendy to arrive to help with the hall tile project. Two pieces of good news awaited her: approval to view the autopsies of Santero and Ackerman and a letter from the penitentiary. Sophia had responded to Julie's request for a meeting with, "Not yet, dear, but soon."

Things were looking up. Not that Griffin had anything to do with either of those, but maybe the psychic Francine had the timing lined up at least. Maybe this was a matter of correlation rather than causation. Now if only his grandsonly presence would bring about a magical solution for all the repairs.

A few minutes later, Wendy, laden with grocery bags, navigated her way over the various saws and packs of tiles. Julie took them from her.

Wendy eyed the tools and supplies. "Good lord, I think this pile's grown since I was here last. And why are you still camping out in your living room?"

"I'm not camping out." Julie flung a stray bra into the master bedroom. "It's my living room. I'm living in it."

"What do your gentlemen callers think about this situation?" Wendy hauled Julie's comforter back to the bedroom. "Oh, I forgot. They're not allowed to enter your inner sanctum. That would imply something far too serious."

"You laugh, but I've been stalker free since I instituted that rule."

"Speaking of your inner sanctum, did you see the moving van outside? Looks like your new neighbor is finally moving in."

Julie pouted. "I know. I'm no longer the sole proprietor of my lemon trees."

"Have you met them yet?" Wendy peeked through the blinds overlooking the courtyard.

"Nope."

"Maybe it's a cute guy."

Julie's phone buzzed, and she read the text from Griffin.

Colonel Mustard and Ms. Scarlett in the Billiard Room with the rope. Now that was a good plan.

Heat crept up Julie's neck.

"Yeah," she said, hoping her cousin didn't notice her blush, "because getting involved with someone who lives ten feet from you isn't a recipe for total disaster."

"Killjoy. So, we going to put these power tools to use, or what? I'm in the mood to demolish something."

"Easy there, killer. I'll let you cut the tiles down to size."

"Speaking of destroying, how did that douchenozzle take your dismissal last night?"

"What? Oh, um..." Julie fiddled with the coffeepot. She wasn't sure how to break the news to Wendy just yet. "You mean your dismissal? I think you preemptively took care of that for me." Her laugh came out awkward and stilted. Guilt twisted inside of her.

Wendy set down the tile saw and approached with a look that said she smelled something off.

"What did you do?"

Julie averted her eyes, and coffee grounds spilled over the filter. "Nothing."

Wendy leaned forward, and Julie flushed. Gah, the woman was like a human polygraph.

"I slept with him," Julie blurted. "At Miss Peacock's in the billiard room."

"You what?!" Wendy's eyes went wide and furious.

"He followed along on the tour after you left—"

"And you let him?"

Julie held up a hand. "I thought I could prove him wrong, show him what a great tour company we actually run."

Wendy sighed.

"And only after he promised he wouldn't write anything bad about us again. He's really not so heinous." Julie's mind drifted back to an image of him the night before, doting and affectionate. "He's smart, and he's funny and as obsessed with history as I am. I actually think you'd like him if you didn't already want to cut his head off with a tile saw."

Wendy collapsed onto the couch and chewed her lip.

Abandoning the coffee, Julie dropped onto the cushion next to her. "Do you hate me?" Her voice was small.

Wendy let her head fall back against the cushions and let out a long sigh. "Of course not. But seriously, Jules, that guy?"

Three loud raps rattled the front door.

"Don't tell me you gave the guy your address, too," Wendy said.

"Come on now, let's not get crazy."

"Do you know what this is?" Uncle Rob stood on the front porch, jabbing a finger at the screen of his phone. If the red in his cheeks was any indication, he was whipped up about something.

"That appears to be a smart phone, Uncle Rob. It's like a tiny computer you can fit in your pocket. You can even order pizza on it. You should try it sometime."

"Not the phone, smartass. This." He blustered inside and nearly tripped over a displaced stack of books.

Julie scurried in front of him to clear a path, a sick feeling stirring. Whatever this was, it didn't sound good.

Rob swiped the screen on his phone and read: "Deveauxs' Ghost Tour Almost Makes a Believer Out of Me."

A cold sensation pressed into Julie's chest. Was this a headline from Griffin's blog?

"Now, I thought we issued this guy a refund and sent him on his way, but apparently that was not the case," Rob said.

"But he promised. He promised he wouldn't..." Julie's thoughts raced back to his exact words. He promised he wouldn't post anything negative or anything that would reflect poorly on her family, not that he wouldn't post anything at all. Still, it felt like a betrayal. She'd gotten herself in too deep, and it had muddled all of her thinking.

Wendy's semi-understanding expression vanished.

"Shall I go on?" Rob asked. "'Despite my abysmal experience with Deveauxs' vampire tour, their ghost tour was a colossally pleasant surprise, thanks to New Orleans legends and pop culture expert, Julie Deveaux.'"

Rob continued, and Julie felt a growing sense of dread, even though the piece was thoughtful and detailed and very complimentary. There had to be something else looming at the end for her uncle to be this pissed.

"'Julie was so thorough she even treated me to a private tour of Miss Peacock's to visit with Charlie, the bar's resident spirit. I can't say for sure what I experienced was a ghost, but I felt these legendary cold spots for the first time. And something else I can only classify as otherworldly.'" Innuendo dripped from the last word. Rob shot Julie a pointed look, and Wendy snorted.

Rob's eyes flashed at Wendy. "This is not a laughing matter. Julie, do you know what this looks like?"

She couldn't quite bring herself to meet her uncle's eyes and instead busied herself with the coffeemaker. "Good publicity?" She could think of about three million things, some involving torture, that she'd rather do than talk about her sex life with her uncle, especially when said sex life involved someone he wanted to punch in the face.

"What it's going to look like is that I was so desperate to redeem my business that I sent my niece to put the moves on this guy. What were you thinking, Julie?"

Julie tried to push down the mixture of mortification and anger stirring inside of her. He didn't sound angry now, so much as sad. And more than that, like he felt responsible, like he'd failed her somehow, and this was the consequence.

Julie repeated what she'd told Wendy, minus the sex part. "I think this was his way of trying to do damage control for the vampire tour post." Her voice came out small.

Any remaining fight in her uncle's face cooled, and he rubbed the stubble on his chin. "Julie, I know you always see the best in people, but this guy is bad news. He's hurt our business. He broke his word to you about not posting about us anymore."

He put an arm around Julie's shoulders and squeezed her tight. "I don't usually interfere with your personal life. You're a grown woman, and you can make your own choices, but I'm asking, just this once, stay away from this guy. Please."

Julie's throat tightened. The thought of never hearing another of Griffin's quips or seeing that knowing smile of his produced an unpleasant ache in her chest.

But Uncle Rob was family. He gave and gave and gave and never asked her anything in return. How could she deny him the one thing he'd ever asked for?

Her eyes stung, but she blinked back the ridiculous tears before they could fully form. What was this nonsense? What happened to keeping it casual? With Julie's track record, she'd be running away from him any day now, anyway. Why get more involved when it would only hurt more to extricate herself in the end? Maybe this was for the best.

She gave a tight nod.

Several hours later, Julie stood back to admire her newly tiled bathroom floor. The blue-grey slate gave the place a sleek, modern feel. Her aching limbs and back from the work took her mind off of the impending moratorium on Griffin Durocher.

After thanking Wendy and Uncle Rob profusely and walking them out, Julie swung the wrought iron door closed and sauntered back into the courtyard.

The late afternoon sun streamed through the leaves of the lemon trees and into her eyes, but she still caught the tall silhouette of her new neighbor on the other set of stairs. She squinted at the figure navigating the steps, arms laden with boxes.

"Hello?" she called. Maybe getting to know the new neighbor would be a good antidote to the melancholy that was threatening to set in.

She took a step into the shade, and with the sun blocked, the details of his silhouette filled in. Sweat soaked his white t-shirt and made it cling to the muscles of a familiar back.

Julie did a double take and felt her pulse quicken.

"Griffin?"

From the top of the steps, he shifted the boxes and looked back at her with a quizzical expression.

"What are you doing here?" she sputtered.

"This is my new abode. Well, technically it's an old family place."

Julie's stomach turned over. This whole staying away thing just got exponentially more difficult.

Griffin bent over and shoved one box inside the front door. The view conjured memories of last night, his muscles flexing, his chest pressed against hers. She banished the memory and fanned herself.

"Is this where you live?" he asked.

Julie retreated up her own staircase and nodded.

Griffin shook his head in wonder. "Want to come over and see my new place? We could build a fort out of moving boxes." His smile aroused a pang of longing.

"I, uh, I can't right now." Julie fumbled the door open. "I have a thing. Something I have to do for my uncle and my cousin."

"Okay then. Later?"

She met his eyes with a rueful smile. Though it would probably hurt more, she allowed herself another moment to memorize the kindness in his eyes, the dimples that played at the corners of his mouth. Why did she ever agree to not seeing him?

"Yeah, maybe."

CHAPTER 10

For three days, Julie successfully managed radio silence. No return texts, no visits. She'd picked up extra shifts at work, kept Uncle Rob happy, and worked on her thesis.

It hadn't been easy avoiding her next-door neighbor, but she could manage if it meant keeping her family happy, even if her own heart felt as crumbly and broken down as the pieces of the inexpertly cut tile she had to throw out over the weekend.

She'd even waited until she heard Griffin go out the day before to sneak over and leave The Skeptics' Guide on his front step. Relinquishing that last piece of him left a dull ache inside of her that wouldn't seem to go away.

Tuesday, her day off, had started with a particularly sweet text. Dammit. Why was this so hard? He was just a guy. And guys were trouble.

Julie tried for the fifth time to focus on her case file, but everything was addled in her brain. What she needed was something to do with her hands. She had all the ingredients to make her famous étouffée, but everyone she knew was working. It would be a shame to let that go to waste. This was a situation that called for some homemade lemonade.

A glance at the pitiful lone lemon in her stash told her she'd have to chance a trip to the courtyard. Though she should've checked for signs of Griffin, tiptoeing around and staying out of her favorite part of her place was getting old. Wicker basket in hand, she swung the door open.

And almost ran smack into Griffin.

Julie yelped in surprise. Instead of his usual khakis and button-up shirt, he sported dark jeans and a black t-shirt that made him look even sexier than she remembered.

"Hi," he said.

"What are you doing here?"

"Good to see you too."

Julie cringed. "Sorry. Not what I meant."

Griffin ran a hand through his wet hair, sending the crisp scent of pine wafting off of him in waves. He must've been fresh from the shower. The thought of Griffin standing under the steaming jets of water sent her thoughts in dangerous directions.

"I was just coming to check on your phone. I've been sending you texts and you haven't replied, so I just wondered if maybe your charger broke or you dropped it in the sink or something."

"Gah, no, sorry. I've just been really busy." She pulled the door shut behind her and trotted down the stairs.

"I thought we had a good time the other night." He followed her into the courtyard to the cluster of enormous lemon trees. "Not just post-ghost hunting. Everything that came before that, too."

Heat crept up Julie's neck, and she pushed to her tiptoes to grab a lemon. She'd already gone through most of the low-hanging fruit. She'd have to find a way to close the gap between herself and something a little loftier.

"Did I do something wrong? Say something to upset you?" Griffin easily plucked a lemon from a higher branch and held it out.

She frowned and grabbed the stepstool from the corner.

"No, no. I had a good time too." She glanced sideways—they were now eye to eye with her on the step stool—and her heart fluttered and then took a nosedive at the sight of Griffin's keen eyes studying her.

"But?" Griffin prompted.

"Who says there's a but?"

"If there's no but, why haven't you come to say hello? Why ignore my texts?"

Julie sighed. Four more lemons plunked into the basket.

"It's just—you living next door, it's a little intense...and that article you wrote."

Griffin slid his hands into his pockets, and a frown creased his brow.

"Now my uncle thinks I whored myself out to drum up good PR."

"Whoa."

"Yeah."

"I'm sorry if I made it worse. Looks like I should've been more careful with my wording."

She nodded.

"I just—you were so upset about the other post. I thought I could do some damage control."

Julie softened. "I know."

Griffin's expression brightened cautiously. They each placed a lemon in the basket at the same time, and Griffin's hand strayed to cover hers. The comfort of his touch, somehow both new and familiar, pulsed through her, but she pulled away.

"My uncle asked me not to see you."

Griffin stepped closer and rested his hands on one of the heavy iron chairs patinaed with age. "Is that what you want?"

Julie's pulse thumped an erratic beat. How could she answer that? Could she trust something so fickle and capricious? "No. But I just don't know if I can do this."

Griffin's eyes clouded, but he managed a smile again. It was one she'd never seen before, bittersweet and breathtaking.

"Okay," he said.

Julie's heart sank. "Okay?"

"Can't say I'm not disappointed, but I won't push you if that's not what you want."

"Oh."

"But given that we're now neighbors, we should probably still try to be neighborly."

"Neighborly. Yes." Julie added two more lemons. She had plenty, but stopping now would mean ending the conversation, and that didn't seem like an excellent outcome.

"So, neighbor, I watched an excellent documentary last night on Alexander Hamilton and Aaron Burr. Spoiler alert: one of them dies at the end."

"Spoiler alert: they're both dead now." Julie smiled, and relief flooded her when Griffin grinned.

"How's the thesis research going?"

"I got a few more leads over the past few days." She still hadn't shared the topic of her project with him.

"That's good."

"How's the big Halloween ghost-busting project?"

"I don't know. Nothing big enough's coming to mind. I thought about the time warp in City Park, but—"

A gushing hiss exploded from above them.

Julie's gaze whipped in the sound's direction. Water sprayed in noisy spurts from the open master bedroom window.

"Did you leave the shower on?" Griffin asked.

"Shit." Julie took the stairs two at a time, Griffin keeping up behind her.

In the master, water gushed from a busted pipe in the ceiling. Panic leaped inside her. Yet another thing in her life turned upside down and spinning out of control.

Julie shaded her eyes from the torrent of water and lunged to rescue some papers in the corner and a trinket that had been her mother's.

Griffin jumped into the fray and got pelted by side spray as he cleared another stack of books from the side table. "Where's the water main?"

Over the hiss of the water, his words were barely audible.

Griffin asked again and took off in the valve's direction while Julie scrambled through the room, rescuing soggy books, papers, and soaked clothing.

A few minutes later, the gush slowed to a trickle and finally stopped altogether.

Julie squished through the swamp-like carpet, her brain swirling in panic at how much extra work this particular piece of chaos was going to add to her remodeling project. Awesome. But hey, if times got tough, maybe there would be a market for a swamp tour of her master bedroom.

Griffin returned and joined her in spiriting furniture out of the soggy space.

"You got a dry place to put these?" he asked, hefting one of the bedside tables.

"Extra bedroom down the hallway past the living room."

Julie balanced two of her dresser drawers, one spilling over with lacy bras, and followed. "You really don't have to do this. I can manage."

Griffin shook his head. "I don't mind."

They continued lifting and carrying and shimmying the dresser until only the soggy carpet and impossible-to-remove bed remained. While Julie definitely could have handled this on her own, she had to admit it was nice to have someone jump in and help.

"The bedside tables and dresser are salvageable if we get some fans on them fast," Griffin said. "I've got one of my dad's company trucks downstairs. There might be some industrial-strength fans in there."

"I owe you big time."

Griffin grinned and scrubbed a hand through his own wet hair. "I'm afraid this mattress has seen its last days, though."

"Good riddance." Julie stripped off the soggy sheets and hefted the mattress and all of its bad memories onto its end.

"If only the stupid frame would rot enough to fit through the door."

After we set the fans up and the awful mattress rested on the curb, Julie said, "You're a lifesaver. Seriously, if you weren't here, I'd be knee-deep in pipe water and still trying to wiggle that dresser through the door."

Griffin slid to a sitting position on the kitchen tile, wet shoes squeaking. "Just being neighborly."

"Neighbors lend each other cups of sugar. I think this is above and beyond the call of neighborly duty."

"Well, come over with a cup of sugar any time."

Julie smiled at him. "Can I at least offer you a beer in thanks?" She grabbed two Abitas from the fridge.

"I will gladly take you up on that." He produced a key chain bottle opener.

"So, neighbor...." Griffin grinned. A rivulet of sweat trailed down his neck as he took a drink. Julie had to stifle the urge to trace its path with her fingertips. God, why did he have to be so appealing?

"Yes, neighbor?" She barely kept her voice from cracking.

"Can I ask you something?"

She slid down and rested her back against the cabinets next to him. "As long as it's neighborly." She nudged his arm with hers, and sparks stirred along her damp skin. She should probably move farther away.

"What's the deal with the mattress hate?"

Julie took a drink and shrugged. "You know how they're supposed to double in weight every seven years from dead skin and stuff?" She let out a strained laugh.

"And the disdain for that bedroom, in general. I couldn't help but notice that you had a sleeping setup on the couch there."

"That. Oh, I... yeah." Julie cursed herself for not cleaning up. But how was she supposed to know she'd have company? "You're very observant. Speaking of observant, did you happen to notice my lucky Scully Pops doll? I haven't seen that in forever."

"You don't want to talk about it. Message received," Griffin said.

"No, it's just, there's some unpleasant history in there. I don't like to think about it, much less talk about it."

"Ghosts of boyfriends past?" Griffin's shoulder pressed into hers and, God help her, she didn't pull away.

"God, no. Nothing like that. I actually don't bring guys here." She peeled at her beer label. "Ever."

"You've never brought a guy here?"

She shrugged.

His lips turned up into a smile. "How come?"

"If I had a therapist, she'd probably say it's because of the same reason I hate that room. Can we talk about something else?"

Griffin stretched his long legs out in front of him. "I have a room like that, too."

"Yeah?"

"A whole house, actually. Which was probably pretty obvious on the tour the other night."

Ah. That house.

"You've probably pieced it together, but Sophia was my grandmother. I've only been back once since the...since they locked her up. Since she pleaded no contest."

Julie didn't miss the note of bitterness that accompanied the last words.

"That must have been awful," Julie murmured. "Must still be. I'm sorry."

"Yeah." His Adam's apple bobbed. Unlike the other night, no stony expression masked the flash of pain in his eyes.

Trying not to think about the line she was crossing, Julie rested a hand on his leg. He covered hers with his own, and their fingers threaded together.

"There was this little hideaway closet I played in when I was a kid, right off of the parlor. The ceiling was only four feet tall, but my grandma would climb inside and play pirates or colonial occupation with me." His eyes took on a wistful tint. "But when I went back, even that felt wrong. Like I couldn't be sure if even the happy memories were part of some elaborate hoax."

Griffin let loose a long, slow exhale. Cicada songs filled the silence. "This person I remember who tucked me in and read me stories and played pirates with me wasn't who I thought she was at all." He shook his head. "I wouldn't wish that feeling of betrayal on anyone."

Julie leaned her head on his shoulder. "And that's why the blog," she mused. His unrelenting drive to preemptively out frauds.

"I guess. Yeah."

Julie squeezed his hand. They sat there in silence, leaning on each other for a few moments before she spoke. So many other questions bubbled up after this new understanding: about his childhood, about his grandmother, but asking any of them felt like crossing a dangerous line. Even if she didn't want to ask them as Julie the researcher, to Griffin, the grandson of her thesis subject, the landscape of those questions was fraught with land mines. How would he react if he knew she was studying his grandmother? Would everything they shared feel like a hoax?

The worry turned inside of her like a restless sleeper. He returned her squeeze, and she tried to concentrate on the way his rough palms felt against her skin. The sensation was anchor and flight all at once. Despite her own guarded, easily spooked heart and the potential rift with her uncle, she couldn't seem to stay away from Griffin. She wanted to stay like this, to be Julie and Griffin, kindred spirits who liked weird historical facts and laughed at each other's jokes. Her body craved another look of unguarded adoration from those green eyes of his. She wanted to feel the long-disused door to her heart crack open and let more light in. But getting deeper into the subject of his grandmother reminded her that whatever else they were to each other, they were still also Julie, the researcher and Griffin, grandson of Sophia Durocher. Eventually, that could blow up and bring an end to all of this.

"Well, this has turned cheery," she said.

Griffin laughed, and his shoulder shook against hers.

"I was planning an X-Files marathon for later tonight," Julie said. "But I could put it on now. Alien abductions, mystical creatures, gruesome, supernatural deaths. Always peps me right up."

"As much as I would like that, I'm dying for some dry clothes and a shower."

Julie's heart gave a sad twist. "Oh, okay. Sure."

Griffin rose, and she followed him to the door.

"Thanks again for all of your help today."

"Any time." He looked back at her like he was about to say something else but turned and headed down the stairs instead.

She wanted to ask him to come back after his shower, but she was so unused to extending an invitation like that. Even more unused to being invested in the answer. The words stuck in her throat.

"I guess I'll see you around," she said instead.

He walked away, and the strength of her desire to see him walking back the other direction again hit her in the gut and overpowered her common sense.

"Hey, Griffin—" Her pulse tripped.

He turned, the afternoon sun casting his gorgeous frame in a stark and peaceful relief.

"I was thinking of making some étouffée later. You wouldn't want to come back and have some with me, would you? Maybe a side of aliens too?"

She had just willfully invited a guy into her home. Julie's stomach did a nervous somersault.

A slow, sexy smile spread across Griffin's face. "Did you just invite me over? To the place where you've never invited any guy?"

She flushed, but nodded.

"How can I say no to that?"

CHAPTER 11

"That étouffée was amazing," Griffin said.

"Well, it should be. It has four sticks of butter in it."

"I think butter is my favorite food group." Griffin shook the suds off his hands.

"You really don't have to do that," Julie said for the third time, but she had to admit, Griffin sudsing up the dishes here in her kitchen was doing all sorts of things for her. Especially with the last dusky lights of twilight winking out and a soft breeze drifting through the open window. It was weird having someone else in her space besides family members, but also...nice. With his laughter and his presence, she didn't have time to focus on the past or the feeling of being out of place in her own home.

She just had to remember they were keeping things neighborly.

"My mom would give me a stern talking-to if I abandoned my manners. My grandmother too."

His carefree expression tightened at the mention of Sophia, and Julie felt a pang.

"So, you're close with your parents?" she said in an effort to steer the conversation into happier waters.

"Yeah. They live uptown, so I get to see them pretty often. My dad most often since I work for his construction company. Mom's a lawyer, mostly construction law."

"Is that how they met?"

Griffin nodded. "She represented him and ended up saving his business. Then he asked her out every day until she said yes."

"They're still together, then. Must be nice." Julie bit her lip.

"Yeah. What about you? You close with yours?"

"My mom, yeah. It was just the two of us for most of my childhood. She's kind of like my older, less jaded twin. If my twin wore pastel dresses and was always on a sugar rush."

Griffin studied her with a gaze that set her off-kilter with its unabashed affection. This sort of thing was going to make keeping up the friendly neighbor thing much more difficult.

Flustered, she rambled on. "She's the strongest person I know. It always blows me away how she can be so darn trusting and hopeful after everything she's been through. She's like a walking Hallmark movie or something."

"What about your dad?"

"Oh, he's more of an HBO movie. Addiction, abandonment. But awesome soundtrack, so there's that."

Her voice came out light and flippant, but her jaw twitched, and she could feel the sting of the long-ago venom seeping back into her being, threatening to ruin an otherwise fun and distracting night.

Griffin gave a commiserating frown and opened his mouth.

"So, X-Files?" Julie attacked the counter with a sponge and Griffin's brow furrowed. Damn. She always did this, shut down whenever the conversation turned to Very Important Things.

"Sure, why don't you get it ready and I'll check and see how your furniture's drying out."

A few minutes later, Griffin joined Julie on the couch. Though his arm rested near her shoulder, he was still farther away than she would've liked. Then again, she did give him the whole "we can't do this" speech earlier today. He was infuriatingly good at respecting boundaries, apparently. Julie passed the edge of the comforter to him and scooted in, but he still kept a respectable cushion-length away.

"What's the prognosis?" she asked.

"Minimal water damage. Looks like they survived. Ooh, is this the one with the shape shifters? I love this one."

"You'll have to be more specific. There was a lot of shifting of shapes on this show."

"The one with the Indian reservation?"

Julie smiled. "This is the episode that got me hooked. Some of the other season one stuff was iffy, but by this one I couldn't stop watching."

"Come on. Mulder and Scully in that hotel room in the first few episodes where she thinks she has the same mark as the victims? That analytical, skeptical perspective of hers. Admit it, that keen logical reasoning is hard to resist."

"So is openness to wonder." Julie eyed the center of the couch. The gap between them had shrunken as if they'd unconsciously moved closer to one another.

"Are we still talking about X-Files here?"

Julie's eyes glinted. "Hmm. A skeptic and a true believer. Sounds like an unlikely pairing."

"Worked for Mulder and Scully."

"And you remember which one of them was ultimately right, don't you?"

Griffin rolled his eyes, but his mouth spread into an easy smile, complete with a dimple sighting. His arm brushed her shoulder.

"We should make this into a drinking game," Julie said. "Drink every time one of them takes out one of those breadbox-sized cell phones."

"Or whenever Mulder asks Scully to believe him."

"And whenever there are shoulder pads involved as an unfortunate wardrobe choice."

"Whenever Scully has Mulder's back. Even if she thinks she knows better."

Their eyes held each other's for a moment, and something hummed between them.

"Cell phone!" Julie pointed to the screen. She clinked her beer bottle against Griffin's, and he laughed.

The soft chatter of the TV lulled them into a comfortable silence, broken by the occasional shout of shoulder pads! or Scully, you've got to believe me. But Julie's mind wandered back to the way Griffin had her back today. Even when she'd dodged his calls. Even when she'd tried to end things. She expected everyone to eventually run away, yet here he was, wading through wet carpet to save her belongings despite her efforts to push him away. Despite all reason.

"It was my parents'." Julie swallowed and nodded to the doorway. "The bedroom."

Griffin shifted until their bodies nearly touched.

"I was eight when they split up, but even then I knew it was better than all the fighting. I remember hiding in my closet with my headphones on, waiting for it to be over. And my mom just took it. Kept thinking it would get better. Until he drained all of our savings and took off one day."

The comforting weight of Griffin's arm slid across her shoulder.

"We would've lost this place if not for Uncle Rob and Aunt Jacqui. They took out a second mortgage to help keep us afloat."

"I'm sorry. That must have been awful."

"The crazy thing is I thought it would get better after that—finally peaceful, you know? And I guess it did for a while. But then the boyfriends started. They were in and out of that room too, each one more loser-y than the last. I think she just wanted someone to love her, but they all left eventually. A particularly pond-scummy one even stole our antique china on the way out."

Griffin squeezed her shoulder. The confession stirred up the old cocktail of pain and shame that burned her from the inside out — she'd watched her mom get hurt repeatedly by men she put her trust in, and Julie'd never been able to protect her. But something about saying the words aloud, here in the dark, nestled close to someone else who knew a thing or two about troubled pasts, leeched some of the poison out of the memories.

"When my mom moved out, this place was paid off. I thought I could remodel a little, make a fresh start. I repainted that bedroom and moved all my stuff in there, but I just couldn't..." A lump formed in Julie's throat. "I couldn't sleep there. Too many ghosts of those memories still there."

Her chest felt shaky and vulnerable. Like by saying these things to Griffin, she'd just lifted a weight that she was simultaneously accustomed to and weighed down by. She pulled her knees to her chest and leaned on his shoulder.

"What was your remodeling plan?" Griffin asked.

"Turn that room into a study/guest room and knock out the wall between the two tiny bedrooms on the other side."

"Not a bad idea."

"Yeah?" Julie smiled. "As you can see, it's slow going with a limited budget and limited construction know-how. And then there's that god-awful 300-pound bed frame in there. My dad built it inside the room, and it won't fit through the door no matter how hard I try. So until I can afford to have that wall knocked down, I'm stuck with it." Julie sank back against the cushion.

Griffin's eyes glittered. "Maybe not."

Julie arched an eyebrow.

"I have an idea. And some construction know-how. And some tools. Be right back."

He returned several minutes later with an axe, a tool that resembled Thor's hammer, and something called a stud finder.

"I feel like there's a 'stud already found' joke in here somewhere." Julie smiled.

Griffin ran the stud finder along the wall. "Good news. You've got two extra feet of wall before you hit anything important. So the question is, do you want to hack up the bed frame or the wall? Or you could always go for both. Why let the catharsis end with one?"

Julie spun the handle of the sledgehammer, the thrill of possibility humming through her. But even though this wall was holding her back, it was also stabilizing her, keeping her in a familiar place. Breaking out of that would hurt like hell, even if it moved her forward.

"Am I going to be able to lift this, or is it only for the worthy son of Odin?"

"It came from Home Depot, not Asgard, so you're probably okay."

She moved on to the axe and tested its weight. "I'm not sure I can be trusted to use this without sending myself to the hospital."

"Hey, it was just an idea. We don't have to do this if you don't want to." Griffin must've sensed her uncertainty.

Heart thumping, she walked into the bedroom and rested the axe blade on the footboard. Griffin was right. She didn't have to do this. She could keep the status quo and go on in her holding pattern. Everything would be familiar and okay. Or...

Or she could finally take a strike at these things that had been holding her back. Leave okay in the dust and take a chance on brilliant and unknown.

She sucked in a deep breath.

"I'm a fast learner if you can show me some safety precautions."

After being fitted with safety goggles and gloves, and some coaching from Griffin that would let her do the job without ending up with a peg leg, Julie let the axe fly.

Her swing rent the air, and the blade bit into the bed frame with a satisfying thunk. Wood chips arced through the air. At the sight of the decent-sized crack she'd made with her own two hands, a giddy laugh bubbled up.

"I think I've found my calling."

Griffin joined in her laughter. "Now try to hit the same spot again."

She did. With every swing and splinter, she chipped away at the anchors of her past. Those nights hiding in the closet while her parents screamed their heads off. The nights her mom cried herself to sleep and Julie climbed into bed next to her and stroked her hair, helpless to take the pain away. This swing for Larry. Another for Fred. And one for Case, the china thief. A dismantling blow for her father, who promised to love her and take care of her and instead left without saying goodbye. Her limbs sang with freedom. So many times she'd felt powerless to help, but every plank she tossed out the window gave her back some of that power.

Griffin joined in and cracked the headboard.

"Timber!" he yelled.

Together they heaved it out the open window and let it shatter to pieces on the courtyard below. Julie gave the sledgehammer a whirl. When they let the last pieces fall, she wiped the sweat from her brow and looked back at the empty room, feeling a thousand pounds lighter, like she might float away if she didn't have something here to anchor her.

"Feel better?" Griffin asked.

"Oh, yeah." Julie pulled off her gloves and studied him. Sweat dripped down his temples, and his chest rose and fell with the exertion of helping her decimate her burdens. What an unexpected gift this whole day had been. What an unexpected gift the entirety of his presence in her life had been.

Julie slipped an arm around his waist.

"For the record, you look really hot wielding a sledgehammer." Griffin's breath tickled her ear.

She nudged him, a sly smile playing on her lips.

"For the record, so do you. Very Aasgardian, even."

Julie leaned into the comforting weight of him, letting him anchor her in this moment. She had her blank page. Her fresh start. Now she just had to have the courage not to screw it up.

"Thank you. That was... I needed that." Her eyes stung.

Griffin wiped hot tears that leaked from her eyes. He pulled her close, stroking her hair, rubbing circles into her back, just holding her as time stretched out and moonlight shone through the open window.

Reveling in the fragile wonder of the newly carved-out space, Julie's heart pounded. She was done resisting. She tilted her head until their gazes tangled and breaths mingled.

"Just so we're clear, are we still just being neighborly?" Griffin asked.

Julie smiled against his lips. "I think I've officially changed my mind about that."

CHAPTER 12

"I could get used to this, too," Griffin said. Several hours later, on the pull-out couch, Julie snuggled closer and laid her head on his bare torso, reveling in the rise and fall against her cheek and the feel of skin on skin, the warmth and connection from head to toe.

The soft lights of the TV danced in the background, and Julie called out, "B-8."

Griffin groaned and plunked a red peg into the game board balanced on his torso. "You sunk my battleship."

"Yes!" Julie propped her head on her elbow. "I am the queen of naked Battle-ship. And we really need to work on your accidental innuendo."

"Who said it was accidental?" He kissed her forehead and moved the game board to the side table. "I've got an idea." Griffin rose, giving Julie an eyeful of his spectacular lean-muscled body, and returned with a familiar blue-jacketed book.

"I thought I gave that back."

"Thought you might want to hang onto it a while longer."

Warmth flooded her chest.

"How far did you get before you returned it?"

Reaching over and flipping through the pages, she felt a swell in her chest at the sight of his now-familiar handwriting in the margins. He wasn't returning hers. He wanted her to have this piece of himself a while longer. Until their bodies aligned again, she inched closer, and she kissed his shoulder.

"I stopped right about here."

"I read a little farther—"

"Overachiever."

"Yep. But, I don't mind rereading."

"I'm afraid I won't like it as much without your running commentary in the margins."

"Now you've got the live version." He slid his glasses back on and cleared his throat. "Chapter 17: On Continued Reflection of Otherworldly Phenomenon and Dealing with Internal Resistance."

"Ooh, just what you need." Julie gave him a playful poke.

"Look who's talking. I believe you're just as acquainted with internal resistance as I am."

"You really want to say that after you've seen my sledgehammer skills?"

"I retract my previous comment."

"Can we read now?"

"Of course, if you're finished interrupting. As I was saying..."

Julie blinked awake to the sound of the bedsprings creaking next to her. Morning already? She must've dozed off while Griffin was reading. The warm fuzzy feeling returned at the memory of lying in his arms, reading and philosophizing into the wee hours.

She reached for him and came up with nothing but the crisp cool of the sheet. Blinking again, she caught sight of him pulling his t-shirt over his head in the pale moonlight.

"Hey, what are you doing?" she asked. "Pressing business with a vampire?"

Griffin started, then sank back down onto the bed and pressed a soft kiss to her lips.

"Caught me. The call of the sparkly ones is strong."

A crease formed between her brows.

Griffin stroked her cheek. "Earlier you said you never had guys over. And with everything that happened with your mom, I get that. So I didn't want you to wake up with a strange guy in your bed eating your leftover étouffée and reading your books if you weren't ready for that."

"You're not a strange guy. Okay, maybe a little strange." She gave him a sleepy smile. "But my kind of strange."

"I think there was a compliment in there somewhere." He nuzzled her cheek and kissed her once more.

"So, until tomorrow?"

"Yes, I guess that would be sensible."

The air cooled in his wake as he stood and slipped his belt through the loops. Already she missed the heat of him next to her, the comfort of having someone who got her jokes and sent smart quips right back at her, and sacrificed his whole day helping her deal with a faulty pipe and her daddy/remodeling issues.

Usually, she couldn't wait to part ways and get back to the cool control that she craved after the heat and rush of bodies, but this felt like something that went far beyond a fleeting rush of pleasure.

Her thoughts swam, her desire for him to stay butting up against her resistance.

He pressed one more lingering kiss to her lips and stepped over the tools on the way to the door.

"Hey, Griffin," she called out before she lost her nerve. Her heart did a series of nervous flips. "Stay."

His smile softened, and the sleep mussed hair made him a glorious sight.

"I mean, if you want to, I'd like it if you stayed."

"You sure about that?"

She nodded. She'd never been so sure of anything in her life.

"We'd have to discuss your hogging of the covers." He grinned. "But I'd like that very much."

CHAPTER 13

"You know, they say the way to a man's heart is through his stomach, but I'm starting to suspect the way to mine is through these pancakes." Julie lounged in her dining room chair and stabbed another forkful of Griffin's creations.

Sunlight streamed in through the kitchen window, casting the copper fixtures of her kitchen in a hazy glow. Griffin flipped another panful of flapjacks and gazed at her, his green eyes soft and bright.

"So what's on your agenda for the day?" she asked.

"I've got to work on a project with my dad in a few hours, and I should catch up on some reading for one of my classes, but that's about it. You?"

"I need to follow up on a few things for my thesis, and then I've got tours tonight. No rest for the wicked."

Her phone buzzed, and an email notification from Miranda popped up. "Speaking of my thesis, message from my advisor."

The golden glow of the past twenty-four hours faded like a mirage as she read and reread the words to make sure she'd understood them right.

"That doesn't look like a happy message face." Griffin settled into the chair beside her. "This looks like a job for extra maple syrup."

Stomach churning, Julie pushed her plate away.

"Uh oh. Something maple syrup won't fix. That must be serious."

Julie blew out a breath. "The dean's been putting a lot of pressure on my advisor, questioning the academic nature of the projects he's been seeing."

"But yours is academic, isn't it?"

She was going to have to tell him. About her research and his grandmother. Her stomach thrashed like a stormy sea.

"The phrase 'sensationalist tabloid fodder' was used." Julie raked a hand through her hair, wounded pride and anger and dread warring inside her.

"Yikes."

"I mean, we're the One week to substantiate my claim or I have to switch topics. So much research—poof. And I'll let down the person I was trying to help." Julie let her head fall into her hands.

"If anyone can dig up evidence, I bet it's you." He took another bite of pancakes. "I sort of want to marry these pancakes too. I might have to fight you for them."

He looked up again, and his face fell. His hand slipped over hers. "I can help if you want, do some digging if the time is an issue."

"You might change your mind."

He leveled an incredulous look at her. "What's this claim?"

And this was where this whole precarious house of cards fell down, wasn't it? Julie swallowed.

"That Sophia Durocher is innocent."

Griffin's hand slid away, and his expression shuttered. "You're studying my grandmother?"

Julie's mouth went dry at the way his voice hardened. He pushed back in his chair, and a barricade cut off the link between them, all steel and barbed wire.

Though she knew from the beginning that he could react like this, she wasn't prepared for the gaping hole it opened in her chest.

"Her whole murder case, yes."

Through the endless silence, Griffin's jaw muscle ticked. She wished he'd say something. Yelling might be better than this awful silence.

"Is that what this is about?" He waved a hand between them and slid his chair away from the table. "I'm just some piece of historical fascination to you? That's a new level of sick."

"No. God, no." Julie reached for his arm.

He snatched it away. "Since I was ten years old, everyone's treated me like some kind of circus freak because of my grandmother. My brother and I got kicked out of our school. My parents lost their clients. I lost all my friends. Then there were these other kids that started lurking around, but it turned out they only wanted to be our friends because we were related to a celebrity murderess. I just didn't expect that from you." He stood, yanked at the collar of his shirt, and fixed her with a flinty gaze.

"I thought for once, I'd found someone who didn't care about that and saw me instead of the grandson of Sophia Durocher. I should've known better."

"Griffin, wait. It's not like that." Panic rising, she followed him as he gathered up his tools and slammed them into his bag. "I do see you. I see the guy who likes the same books as I do and the same nerdy TV shows. And the guy who spent his entire day yesterday hauling furniture and stopping the flood in my apartment and helping me hack up that awful old bed and letting me beat him at naked Battleship."

Griffin folded his arms across his chest, his jaw still ticking, but he'd at least stopped slamming down tools.

"Yes, I'm doing my project on your grandmother. But the reason I didn't bring it up is because I was afraid of this. Never once did I intend to use you as a source. Have I ever asked you a single thing about your grandmother or her case? And if that was all I wanted, I sure as hell wouldn't have risked pissing off and hurting half of my family by seeing you."

His stance lost some of its hard edges.

"I believe your grandmother is innocent, though, and I'd like to prove that." She placed a tentative hand on his arm. "Wouldn't you?"

"Yeah, well, it'd be easier to want that if she wanted it herself. She never even put up a fight."

Julie squeezed his shoulder. "She took the plea bargain for a reduced sentence, Griffin. That's not the same as admitting guilt."

"The outcome was pretty much the same to me."

"Look, I know the fallout hurt you. I can't even imagine what that was like. But from everything I've gathered, she did it because the evidence against her was damning. The alternative was a long public trial that would put her family—put you—through even more misery. Put yourself in her position. If you were innocent, wouldn't you want the people you loved on your side? I don't think you and your brother were the only victims here."

Griffin's jaw tightened again, and he hefted the tools over his shoulder. "I'm glad you have my life figured out. I have to go."

CHAPTER 14

Two days later, Julie squinted at the autopsy reports for Santero and Ackerman and tried to ignore the sting of Griffin's keeping his distance. She'd known this could be a problem, and it sure made it easier to stay in line with what her uncle wanted, but his continued silence hit her in the gut whenever she saw a funny historical meme or heard the hinge squeak of the pull-out couch.

"Look at what's left," she murmured, pushing the thought of him out of her mind. Did that mean something had been there before and been removed? There wasn't any obvious sign of tampering.

Multiple stab wounds all lined up on the right side of the bodies. But what did that prove, except that the killer was a lefty?

She pushed the papers aside and checked her messages again. Nothing.

A knock sounded at the door, and her stomach jumped.

Griffin stood on the landing, his eyes downcast.

Julie hung back.

"I've been thinking." He looked up to meet her gaze. "Maybe you were right. About my grandmother."

The corner of her mouth tugged into the hint of a smile.

"Maybe I blamed all of that stuff that happened to my brother and my parents and me on the wrong person. I want to help."

"Griffin, that wasn't a ploy to get you to help me."

"I know. It's just... if I've been wrong all these years and shut her out over a crime she didn't commit—" He shook his head, the pain fresh and clear in his eyes. "I owe it to her to do whatever I can to set things right."

***

"Are you sure you want to do this?" Julie asked.

Griffin turned the key until the front door of the Sophia Durocher house clicked open.

His jaw tightened, but he nodded. "I should've done this a long time ago."

Julie stepped inside the entryway behind him. The floor plan she'd studied so often she had it burned into her brain came alive in vivid—if dust-coated—color. Her fingers tingled in anticipation.

Though only abandoned for fifteen years, the whole place looked frozen in time far before the twentieth century. Queen Anne chairs with taffeta upholstery and a hand-carved radio cabinet lent the place an air of nostalgia. While she kept her eye on Griffin, ready to exit at any sign that this was too much for him, it was hard not to ogle this place that had lived in her imagination for as long as she could remember.

Griffin blew out a breath as they made their way to the infamous parlor. For him, Julie knew this wasn't just the backdrop for a murder. It was a museum of his childhood snatched away from him far too soon. "She said she had it modeled after a Victorian mansion in when spiritualism was all the rage."

Julie made her way through the reading room, its desk hulking in the center and armoires on the periphery, laden with crystal orbs, porcelain figurines, and framed photos.

"What are we looking for, exactly?" He stepped onto the maroon-colored carpet of the parlor.

"Clues? Anything out of place, I suppose. I think you'd be able to spot that better than me." Julie picked up a photo of a green-eyed boy of five or six covered in paint and clinging to a younger Sophia Durocher. "Wow. Is this you as a little boy?"

Griffin peered over her shoulder, and his expression went nostalgic. "My brother and I got into the garden shed and 'repainted' that day."

"And this is your grandmother?" She picked up another black-and-white photo of a young woman signing a document. The crinkles at the corner of her eyes matched Griffin's.

"Yeah, I think she was signing the papers to buy this place. She was always so proud of owning her own business."

Julie smiled and studied the photograph. Something about it tickled the back of her brain, but she couldn't put her finger on why it seemed important.

Stepping over bloodstains on the carpet, she continued into the room, trying to catalogue all the details, but nothing unusual stood out. Anything suspicious, the detectives had likely taken into evidence.

Griffin stopped in front of a miniature-sized door built into the back wall. His eyes roved the space and clouded over.

Julie slipped a hand into his and squeezed. "Is that your secret hideout?"

"Yeah." He let out a breath and settled on the edge of the desk. "It's weird being here. I was ten last time I was here. So many memories."

"We can go any time you want," Julie assured him.

"No, this is good. It's time I faced it." He ran a hand over the long notepad and porcelain cup of pens and pencils positioned to the right side of the massive cherry wood desk.

Something clicked in Julie's mind. "Look at what's left." Her heart leapt at the memory of the psychic's words.

Griffin furrowed his brow in question.

"I just remembered something from the autopsy. Here. Stand in front of me." Julie positioned a confused Griffin a few paces away. "Just humor me."

After making mock-stabbing motions toward his chest, she let out a squeal of excitement. This is what her subconscious had locked onto when she saw the picture.

"I know I said I was okay with being here, but I'm not sure I'm up for historical reenactments just yet," Griffin said.

Julie skipped back to the mantel and brought the photograph of Sophia signing the mortgage papers back to Griffin. "In the autopsy, nearly all the stab wounds were on the right side of the men's bodies."

"Okay..." Griffin said.

"Look, she's signing with her right hand."

Understanding dawned in Griffin's eyes as they moved from the desk arrangement to the photograph.

"The wounds would be at an unnatural angle for a right-handed person. How could the police have missed that?" The adrenaline rush of a new discovery pulsed through her.

"Because someone had already pleaded guilty."

"And why use police resources to investigate a case that was already closed?" Julie bounced on the balls of her feet. "It's not exactly locking down a new suspect, but it's a start."

CHAPTER 15

The next few days passed in a frenzy. Every moment Julie wasn't giving tours and Griffin wasn't working construction jobs, they spent holed up together trying to clear Sophia's name and save Julie's thesis. Whether in Julie's chaotic apartment or Griffin's sparsely decorated one, they pored over every viable lead on a lefty who had it out for Santero and Ackerman.

Even when they were working up a sweat making repairs at Julie's or working up a sweat in more pleasurable ways, they were two people obsessed.

One evening, on a rare break, Julie and Griffin strolled out of Griffin's favorite praline shop and down Royal Street. Faraway strains of jazz music filled the humid air. Black and orange garlands and cotton spider webs decorated the windows of the French Quarter shops.

Julie finished the last heavenly bite of her chocolate praline and closed her eyes in contentment.

Griffin slipped a hand into hers, and she started. The feel of his work-roughened palm on hers still sent tingles dancing along her senses. For once, even though they were in a very public place with a possible Wendy or Uncle Rob sighting, she didn't pull away.

"It has to be Marie," Julie said. "We keep investigating these other possibilities, but I keep circling back to her. Especially now that we know she worked for Santero and Ackerman and that they roughed her up and treated her like crap."

"I know. Me too," Griffin said. That particular piece of information had come courtesy of Sophia's journal, which Griffin found in a secret spot in the Durocher house. "And her disappearance immediately after is especially shady."

Griffin offered Julie the last bite of his praline, and she let the sweet chalky pecan goodness melt on her tongue.

"Sharing the last of your chocolate, now that is—" Love, she started to say, but choked back the word. Heat flushed her face, and her inner panic alarm sounded. Where had that come from? And anyway, that was insane. She'd only known the guy for what, a few weeks? Love was definitely not in the equation.

"That's what?" Griffin asked.

"That's... what I'm talking about," Julie finished lamely.

"Julie, what a nice surprise!" Before Julie knew what was happening, her mom enveloped in her an unmistakable full body hug. After a moment, her mom pulled back, but her gardenia perfume lingered. Today her mom was clad in a lavender tube dress and matching heels. She had the doe eyes and dewy complexion that gave the impression that she might possess a secret cadre of animated woodland creatures.

Those doe eyes locked onto Griffin's and Julie's linked hands, and a smile that was at once devilish and motherly broadcast across her face.

"Mom, this is my... Griffin. Griffin, my mom, Angeline."

"Well, my, my. You must be someone special, Griffin. It's not often our Julie meets a young man she sees fit to bring out in public."

"Mom." Julie flushed.

"It's nice to meet you," Griffin said.

"And speaking of someone special, there's someone I'd like you to meet too." Angeline bounced on the balls of her feet. "Julie, this is Dean."

Julie's stomach went sour, and her gaze moved to the handsome Black man with salt and pepper hair in khakis and boat shoes standing next to her mother.

"Hey." Julie's jaw tightened.

"Your mom's told me so much about you." Dean held out his hand to shake Julie's. But she only stared at it until Griffin nudged her.

"Hey, we were just going to get some coffee. Would you like to join us?" Angeline asked.

"No," Julie answered at the same time Griffin said, "We'd love to."

"Great. It's settled then." Angeline looped her arm through Julie's and trotted off toward Jackson Square.

Julie glared at Griffin. He threw up his hands with an apologetic look and mouthed, "Come on, it's your mom."

Yeah, Julie thought, and her loser future ex-boyfriend.

CHAPTER 16

"Your mom seems really great," Griffin said later. He and Julie were both poised in front of her computer, navigating the Louisiana name change registry.

"She is. She seemed to like you too."

"I get that a lot." Griffin grinned.

"Yeah, I bet." She gave him a playful nudge. Julie squinted at a record that popped up on the screen and squealed. "Bam! November 2001, Marie Y. Reynard to Carlotta Snow."

Griffin slapped her a high five. Julie bounced to her feet and rolled her tired shoulders.

"This calls for a break and celebration." She slid her arms around Griffin's waist and let her fingers skim the skin under the waistband of his jeans.

His arms wound around her, and he pulled her into a kiss. "It was nice, meeting your mom today."

A brief flutter of nerves winged through her chest as the realization hit her. She'd introduced him to her mother. She could count on one finger the number of guys she could say that for. And she'd been out with him in public. More than twice. And he'd been a regular fixture in her place since the day the pipe burst. This was... something. Possibly she'd been abducted by aliens and replaced with a kinder, less jaded Julie.

"You know, Dean seemed pretty all right too," Griffin said tentatively.

Nothing like talk about Mom's boyfriend to ruin the mood. Julie made a noncommittal sound. "Can we get back to the celebrating?" She pressed her lips to his neck.

"Yes, momentarily." He stroked her cheek and pulled back to look her in the eyes. "You were a little hard on him."

"Yeah, well, I've learned not to get too attached to her future ex-boyfriends."

"I get that. But people change. They make better choices sometimes. You, for example, have recently acquired excellent taste in men."

Julie smirked.

"But what if this is a decent guy who treats her right and makes her happy for a change?"

"He did seem nice." Julie thought about the way Dean had seemed excited about her mother's idea of going back to nursing school and how he'd seemed genuinely interested in getting to know Julie and Griffin. Which is much more than she could say for any of her mom's previous boyfriends. "But statistically speaking, outlook not so good."

"Okay, I concede the point, but you obviously care about your mom. Do you really want to reject someone she cares about without even giving him a chance?"

"Are you trying to tell me you know more about my mom after an afternoon of beignets than I do after a lifetime?" Julie's voice rose. Where was this surge of anger coming from?

"No, of course not." Griffin's voice was gentle. He reached to knead at the knots in Julie's shoulders. She stiffened at first, but then let his touch wear away the tension.

"There's a pattern here. Trust me. Highest highs then crushing lows," she said.

"Only takes one to break the pattern."

Julie leveled a skeptical look at him.

"All I'm saying is things can change. That's the beauty of life. We're not limited to who we used to be."

Julie leaned into his touch, mind swirling with all the changes that had taken place in her own life since Hurricane Griffin made landfall. He'd swept in and shaken up her home, her research project, and her heavily guarded heart. But when the dust settled, and it got scary or uncomfortable, who was to say she wouldn't retreat to her old ways?

"Sure, but history has a way of repeating itself, doesn't it? Patterns hold. We're creatures of habit."

"Yeah, but who says we can't create new patterns?" Griffin brushed her hair out of her eyes. "You aren't limited to who you used to be, either."

She wondered how hard she'd have to fight to make that true.

CHAPTER 17

Julie wasn't sure how, in the span of a week, her apartment had gone from a place that could've doubled as a convent to a place filled with not one, but two sweaty, good-looking guys. But the next morning Griffin showed up on her doorstep, tool box to one side and older brother on the other, looking like archangels of HGTV.

Julie ran a hand over her freshly scrubbed face and smoothed her messy ponytail. "Did I mix up our plans? I thought we weren't meeting until noon."

"Declan had some extra time this morning, so I thought we'd see if you wanted a hand pulling the carpet up in there. It's going to mildew soon if you don't get rid of it."

Julie cast a dismayed look at the week's dishes piled in the sink and the general disorder of the place, but it only took a moment for her to step aside and welcome them in. When Jesus, Mary, and Bob Vila send willing carpet ripper-uppers, you don't send them away, even if you're still in your PJs.

While the Durochers went to work pulling up the carpet, Julie made some coffee and smiled at the easy, competitive banter between the brothers. It reminded her of what she had with Wendy. The thought of her cousin tugged at her guilty conscience. The two shared everything. But she'd yet to come clean about seeing Griffin again. She hated to hide anything from Wendy, but every time she worked up the courage to tell her, she chickened out. Even mentioning it felt like admitting this was something Very Serious. And she wasn't ready to consider that possibility yet.

"Your room is officially denuded," Griffin announced. He and Declan shouldered the thick roll of carpet and pulled it into the hallway.

Julie cracked a joke about the implications of his deflowering her room, but her voice caught as she wandered into the newly bare space. "Wow."

With all the baggage and the history carted away, the place felt raw and invigorated with a new energy. Of course, being stripped down also made the flaws more noticeable.

She eyed the chips in the baseboards and ran a hand along the scuffs on the wall where the headboard used to be. "Kind of banged up."

Griffin came up behind her and circled an arm around her waist.

"Looks pretty good to me. Besides, now comes the fun part."

She leaned back into his chest and nodded. She had to admit, even with all the scratches and dents, the place had good bones. A history of being broken, sure, but something to build on and create something new.

"Julie, you have company," Declan called out from the entryway.

"What's with all the pre-noon visitors today?" Julie walked into the hallway and froze at the sight of her cousin's familiar auburn hair past Declan's shoulder.

"Wendy. Hey." Julie's nerves spiked, and her gaze darted to the doorway where Griffin stood, just out of view.

"Hey." Wendy's smile turned sly and teasing. "I was going to see if you wanted to go to the farmer's market with me, but it looks like you're busy." She gave Declan an appreciative once-over.

Julie flushed. "Busy? No. We," — Julie motioned between Declan and herself—"we are not busy. This is my new neighbor's brother. You know how the pipe burst last week? They were just helping me tear out the carpet."

"I wish I had helpful neighbors. Mine just blast reggae music at two a.m. and steal my garbage cans," Wendy said. "So where's this mystery neighbor hiding?"

Wendy stretched to her tiptoes, and Julie angled to block the path to the hallway. Why hadn't she just told Wendy before?

"Hello again."

Julie's shoulders tensed at the sound of Griffin's voice at her back.

Gaping, Wendy turned an incredulous look on Julie.

"You aren't going to break my foot with a bag of pennies again, are you?" Griffin attempted a smile, but Wendy frosted him out.

"So, obviously you two have already met." Julie sprung forward and pointed Wendy in the other direction. "But you haven't met Declan yet. Declan, my cousin Wendy. Did I mention he's into bad movies too? Wendy goes to those B movies in the park nights every summer."

Wendy gave a tight smile and stomped for the door.

Julie jogged to catch her. "Wendy, wait."

"Did you even try to stop seeing him or did his 'otherworldly' recreational skills fog your brain?" Wendy hissed.

"You told her about that?" Griffin asked from across the room.

"You alluded to it on your blog for the world to see, genius." Julie turned back toward her cousin and hated the hurt she saw in her eyes.

"I did try, but—"

"I get it. You like him. The book and all that." Wendy sniffed and studied her shoes for a long moment. "Were you ever going to tell me? Obviously, this is not a casual thing. He's here in your space. He's introduced you to his brother and you haven't run away screaming."

"Of course I was going to tell you."

"When?"

"When it came up."

Wendy shot her a pointed look.

"Look, you and your dad haven't exactly made it easy."

Wendy sighed.

"Griffin was in the courtyard with me when the pipe burst. He helped me clean up after the flood. That's all."

"That's clearly not all." Wendy shot back, but the words lacked bite, and a ghost of her smartass smile returned.

"Okay, all-knowing one. So we've been spending a lot of time together. He's been helping me with my research. And..." Julie hesitated, heat creeping up her cheeks, "I like him."

As the admission echoed in her brain, Julie felt as if she'd been shoved into a free fall.

Wendy studied Griffin with fresh eyes, like he was some kind of mythical creature she hadn't really believed in and was seeing for the first time.

After a long pause, Wendy said, "Okay, fine. If this is going to happen" — she gestured from Julie to Griffin — "I think we need a trial by fire. I'm sure you won't mind bringing him to family dinner."

"What? No. No, no, no," Julie said. Deveaux family dinners were tumultuous affairs filled with debates and scrutiny of the younger generation's life choices and a rotating guest list of her mom's boyfriends.

"Actually, that's not a bad idea," Griffin said.

Julie goggled at him. "So my uncle can ridicule you? That's a terrible idea."

"I think it'd be nice. Give us a chance to mend fences. Plus, your mom already likes me. Maybe she could help sway your uncle to my side, too."

"He's met your mom?" Wendy's eyes went impossibly wide. "This definitely calls for a family gathering."

Julie's nerves stood at high alert. This was all happening so fast. She wasn't sure she was ready to leave the comfortable little bubble she and Griffin had been in since they'd started seeing each other again. Yes, they'd bumped into her mom and what's-his-face and gone out for coffee together, but that was happenstance. This was a deliberate thing. Dinner with the family. A declaration of serious intent.

Julie watched Griffin chat with a newly receptive Wendy, his disarming grin in place. He was willing to make peace with a girl who had nearly broken his toes with a bag of pennies and to face the gauntlet of fury that was Uncle Rob, all for her. As much as this warmed her, she felt the unsteady sway of uncharted territory. All of her experience said this was practically an invitation to future heartbreak.

Declan slipped out the door with the last of the carpet.

"What do you say?" Griffin asked. He slipped an arm around her waist and pulled her close. "If things blow up, it could still make for a great story."

She leaned into him. The comforting press of his nearness cut through her nerves. Even though her fight-or-flight instincts had already laced up their running shoes and urged her to retreat to safety, the lure of more of this was strong. She pushed through the lightheadedness.

"How does Friday sound?"

CHAPTER 18

Julie slipped into her black dress in the back room of the gift shop after her afternoon tour and blinked against the cloud of vanilla perfume Wendy had just doused her with. All the while, her stomach twisted into knots that would impress a pretzel.

It was Friday. T-Minus two days until Halloween and only hours until the big meet-the-family dinner. Julie had spent most of the day at the library, trying to smother her nerves while typing up her findings.

"Any word from the crankypants advisor?" Wendy asked.

"Keep all appendages crossed the right-handed thing buys me more time." Julie slicked on lip gloss. "Or that Griffin tracks down Marie's real address today."

Wendy frowned. "Promise me you're not just going to go knock on a murderer's door like you're Richard Castle or something."

"I won't." Julie checked her phone again and frowned. She hadn't been able to reach Griffin after he'd left to chase down leads on a Carlotta Snow address.

"Relax." Wendy said. "He'll be there. This was practically his idea, after all."

Julie gave an unsteady smile.

"Honey, you in there?" her mom's voice called from outside the door.

"Just a sec, Mom." Julie slid on her heels and opened the door, suddenly immensely grateful for the press of her mom's hug. She even flashed a polite smile at Mr. New Boyfriend, whom Julie had invited in a fit of good will.

Angeline let out a little squeal. You'd think Julie was about to go to prom or accept the Nobel Peace Prize rather than introduce Griffin to the family over oysters. At least her mom was in her corner. Maybe she could help Griffin win some points with Uncle Rob.

Candlelight glinted off of the silver at the table, and soft jazzy notes played in the background. It would have made for quite the romantic setting, if not for the empty chair next to her.

"Maybe we should just order some appetizers," Julie's mom suggested. "Then Griffin can join us when he gets here."

"Sure." Julie managed a weak smile, but wiped her palms on the linen napkin.

Once she'd downed the last of her water, she checked her phone again. Almost eight. Nearly an hour post-official dinner time.

No messages.

After she cast a panicked glance at Declan, he checked his phone as well and shook his head. "This isn't like him. Something must have come up."

The worry, which had set in after the fifteen-minute mark, crossed the line into full-blown mortification.

Across the table, Uncle Rob glanced at his watch, but, to his credit, kept any smugness he might be feeling to himself.

"Maybe he just got the time wrong, honey," Angeline said.

An hour and a half later, dejected and humiliated, Julie trudged back to her apartment. She should've known better. History repeated itself. People did shitty things. She knew that better than anyone. So why did she delude herself that this would be any different? That he'd be any different, with his sexy smiles, his historical knowledge, and his pancake making. She'd let him in, and he'd gone and done this.

There was no new ending to the story. Only the same hard truth. When you open your heart, you hand someone a sledgehammer to break it into pieces at will.

A dull ache began in her chest, and she fought back the tears that threatened to spill.

By the time she reached the iron gate to their shared courtyard, her hurt had turned to anger. Fists shaking, she stomped up his staircase and pounded on the door.

There was no answer from the darkened apartment.

When she reached her own front porch, she found a basket full of lemons and picked up the folded note set on top.

Julie,

Got a lead on Marie's place. I'm going to investigate this afternoon. Maybe I'll have something to dazzle everyone with by dinner time. My phone is acting up, but can't wait to see you and convince your family of my non-douchebag status tonight.

Griffin

Julie's pulse spiked. This afternoon? That was hours ago. What if he was in trouble? Shame at assuming he'd blown her off came over her in a hot wave. He wouldn't just go knock on this woman's door and start asking questions about his grandmother, would he? Yes, that's exactly what he what he would do. Here she was pouting while Griffin might be tied up in the basement of a known killer. Or worse.

Julie tore into her apartment and fumbled through the files on her laptop with shaking hands. There were three possible addresses they'd considered for Marie Reynard, aka Carlotta Snow. They'd already eliminated one, so that left two places he might be.

She pulled out her phone and scrolled until she found the number she was looking for.

"Declan, I need your help. Griffin's in trouble and I think I know where he is."

CHAPTER 19

I n the passenger seat of Declan's police cruiser, Julie bit the inside of her cheek and prayed that they'd make it to Griffin before any of the horrifying scenarios flitting through her mind became reality.

They made a right, and streetlights illuminated bushy trees between the modest homes.

"There. There's his truck." Julie pointed to the Durocher & Sons logo on the side. Equal parts elation and dread swirled inside her.

"What was he thinking, going in there alone?" Declan shook his head and parked on a side street. "You stay here. I'll go check things out first."

"I'm not staying here." Julie cracked open the door.

"Julie, please. If anything shady's going on, I don't want to put you in danger too."

She sighed and nodded, but as soon as she heard the crunch of his footsteps on gravel a house away, she leaped out of the car and caught up to him just as he rang the doorbell.

"You really shouldn't be here," he said.

"If he's in there, I want to help. Plus, if she makes a confession, I'll be recording." Julie flashed the recorder she used for primary source interviews and tucked it into her pocket.

Declan sighed. "I'm not going to talk you out of this, am I?"

"Nope."

The door cracked open to reveal a petite, dark-haired woman.

"Miss Snow?" Declan flashed his badge.

"Yes." Though she'd only be thirty-five if Julie's calculations were correct, the years had been hard on Marie. Her glossy hair shone in the porch light, and Julie saw the remnants of youthful beauty, but heavy lines etched the corners of her wary eyes.

"We're investigating a missing person and some suspicious activity in the area and have reason to believe this person may be in your house."

Julie caught the flicker of anxiety.

"Must be some mistake. Just me and the cats here." She closed the door, but Declan caught it.

"There's no mistake. We're going to have to search the premises."

Marie frowned, and the lines around her eyes deepened, but Declan's face brooked no argument.

"Well, all right. If you must."

As Marie led them into the living room, Julie's stomach churned. The house was long and narrow, like most of the places uptown, her living room, den, and small kitchen visible in the back. The sparsely furnished living room had more shoes lying around than pieces of furniture.

Marie cast a furtive glance at the single bookshelf nestled under the stairs. A thump sounded from that direction.

"What was that?" Julie asked.

Marie smiled, but her skin paled. "Cats. Would you like some tea? I was about to put some on."

"No thanks," Declan answered.

At the same time, Julie said, "I'd love some." Maybe if she could keep Marie occupied, Declan would have a better chance of finding Griffin.

Declan shot her an incredulous look, but she shrugged it off. He shook his head and kept her in sight while he nosed around the bottom story.

In the kitchen, Marie filled the kettle and turned on the stove—all with her left hand. Gotcha. Julie wandered into the kitchen.

"Are you a cop too?" Marie asked.

"No, grad student. Just on a ride along for some research."

"And what is it you're studying?"

"History. Murders. All that fun stuff."

"What sort of murders?"

Julie's heart pounded.

"Historical New Orleans murders. Like Delphine LaLaurie's." Like yours, she wanted to add.

Marie's shoulders relaxed a bit, and Declan disappeared into the foyer.

Foolish or not, Julie blurted out, "And the Santero and Ackerman murders a few years ago. You ever hear about those?"

Frowning, Marie moved slowly and pulled open a drawer. Her fingers closed around a heavy-bladed knife.

Julie swallowed and backed away a few paces until the counter jarred her spine. Stupid. Stupid. Stupid.

"You chop your own tea leaves?" A nervous laugh escaped.

Marie drew the knife out of the drawer. "What is this really about?"

"What do you mean?" Julie edged out the kitchen door into the dining room. "Declan, how's it coming out there? I could use a hand in the kitchen."

Muffled voices came from the living room, followed by the sound of splitting wood, like a door was being kicked in.

"Took you long enough." The sound of Griffin's voice sent a surge of relief through Julie, and she lunged away from the kitchen. "Griffin?"

"Not so fast." No sooner had Julie made it to the den than Marie wrenched her back, pressing the knife to her throat. Julie's strangled cry died on her lips.

Griffin and Declan stepped over the upturned bookshelf and the fractured door hidden behind it. When his eyes landed on Julie, Griffin sucked in a breath. Despite the fear throbbing through every heartbeat, Julie raked her gaze over Griffin. His movements were slower, clumsier than usual, like someone had drugged him. An angry bruise purpled the skin around his left eye, but other than that, he looked blessedly unharmed. Another rush of shame for doubting him overtook her.

"What did you say your name was, officer?"

"Officer Durocher, ma'am."

"I thought so. Pity. I never thought I'd have to do this again." The blade vibrated against Julie's throat. "But I disappeared and remade myself once. I can do it again."

Declan's hand moved to his weapon.

"Ah, ah, ah. Just so you know, I could slit her throat before you could even get close to taking a shot."

"Don't hurt her." Griffin's voice went low and dangerous.

"Put the knife down, Miss Reynard, and we can discuss this calmly," Declan said.

Though she could scarcely breathe, Julie inched a hand into her pocket and engaged the recorder. If she was going to die here, she could at least do a good deed and set an innocent woman free as her final act.

But how could she signal to Griffin that she was looking for a confession?

Griffin's horror-struck eyes followed the movement of her hand, and he raised an eyebrow. Centimeter by centimeter, she slid the recorder into view until understanding dawned on his face.

"Let her go. Please." The way Griffin's voice broke on the last word undid her. "This is between you and the Durochers, Marie. She has nothing to do with it."

"Then perhaps you shouldn't have dragged her into this."

The four of them stood there in stalemate. The adrenaline in Julie's body rocked her limbs.

The shrill tea kettle whistle broke the silence, and Julie sucked in a breath.

"One of you turn that off." Marie's voice pitched high and manic.

No one moved. The sound pounded, endless, blocking out all thought and matching the keening of Julie's inner screams.

"Fine. She'll do it."

The knife bit into Julie's skin as Marie spun her toward the kitchen. A single drop of blood trickled down her neck, and Julie let out a whimper.

Marie's hand stopped shaking when Julie turned off the burner. "Much better. Now, how are we all going to get out of this little predicament?"

Julie screwed up the last of her courage. "How did she overpower you?" she asked Griffin.

"She put something in my tea. Probably what she did to our grandmother and those two men fifteen years ago. Isn't that right, Marie?"

"Yes, well, sedatives do tip the balance of power in one's favor."

Not exactly a confession, but moving in the right direction.

"Speaking of which, who'd like some tea now? I think this will make what I have to do now less painful for all of us."

The sight of teacups and the bag of white powder Marie lined up on the counter made Julie's knees sway. They had to get out of this.

"Why'd you do it?" Griffin asked.

"Why did I do what?" Marie asked, like it wasn't the most obvious question in the world.

"Kill those men. Let our grandmother go to prison for what you did."

"Well, I'd tell you, but then I'd have to kill you." Marie laughed, a high tinkling sound, and waved the knife in Griffin's direction. "But since you've forced my hand by showing up and getting the police involved, that's the plan anyway, so I suppose it won't hurt anything. Shame. I really will miss this house. Maybe I'll go somewhere with nice beaches next. I hear Florida's nice."

"Why?" Griffin asked again. He edged closer to the stove and locked eyes with his brother. Declan gave a brief nod.

"They were awful men." Marie's knife flashed inches from Julie's face. "They picked me up off the street and forced me into prostitution when I was fifteen.

Fifteen. Then they'd go dress up with the fancy folks and do their politicking. Every time I tried to leave, they'd rough me up so I couldn't get work anywhere else and had to come back to them. They were scum. Lower than scum."

Julie felt a pang for the younger Marie, whose warped sense of right and wrong had been shaped by those bastards.

"But why frame Sophia? What did she ever do to you?" Julie asked.

Marie let out a rueful sigh. "Nothing. Not a damn thing. Just provided me with the perfect cover. It's a shame, really. Just like this business with y'all."

The next succession of events happened in such a blur that Julie scarcely had time to register. Griffin grabbed the teakettle. With eerie precision, he heaved scalding water at Marie's head. Screams erupted, and a sizzling splash seared the back of Julie's scalp.

At the same instant, Declan wrested the knife from Marie's grasp, sending it spinning in a silver whirl across the floor. Julie lunged out of the way of a screaming Marie and into Griffin's arms.

His arms locked around her shaking form, holding her, kissing her, stroking her hair. She'd never felt so happy to be squeezed so tight. "Are you all right?"

She nodded into his chest and pressed as close to him as she could manage. "You?"

"I am now."

"Marie Reynard, also known as Carlotta Snow—" Declan secured handcuffs on Marie's wrists "—you're under arrest for the murders of R.A. Santero and Nicholas Ackerman and the kidnapping of Griffin Durocher, and the attempted murder of Julie Deveaux."

CHAPTER 20

Three weeks later, Julie sat surrounded by the cozy wood and flannel decor of Griffin's parents' living room, nerves aflutter as she awaited Sophia's arrival. Thanks to Marie's recorded confession, Sophia's fifteen-year stint in prison had come to a close, and today she was coming home.

Julie smoothed her skirt and tried to stop the leg she'd crossed over from bouncing with nerves. "Maybe I shouldn't be here. This is a family thing. I should go. I'll meet her soon enough."

Griffin pushed his glasses up the bridge of his nose for the fifth time in as many minutes, his own nerves making a showing, and placed a steady hand on Julie's knee. "You're the reason she's out in the first place. She'd never let me hear the end of it if you weren't here. Besides, I'm excited to introduce her to my girlfriend."

Julie leaned her head on his shoulder, letting a warm tingle flood through her. She was still getting used to this commitment thing, but finding she rather liked it.

Keys rattled in the front door, and Griffin's knuckles went white on Julie's knee. She covered his hand with hers.

Fifteen years of hurt and misunderstandings would take time to heal.

"What if she hates me? What if she doesn't want to see me?" he'd asked Julie earlier.

Julie doubted that was the case. With family, even the deepest rifts could be healed with time.

The door swung open, and Griffin's throat bobbed. Julie squeezed his hand.

In walked the woman Julie had been studying with such fervor since she could remember. Grey now threaded her brown hair. She wandered inside with new freedom of movement. Her eyes took in the house and wrinkled at the corners.

Declan wrapped her in a hug, and she let out a childlike laugh.

Still wrapped in her oldest grandson's embrace, Sophia's eyes settled on Griffin and softened. They drank him in like he was an object of pure wonder that she wanted to memorize every detail of. The love in that look flooded Julie with affection for the woman.

Julie nudged Griffin, and she felt his slow intake and exhale of breath before he rose.

When Griffin crossed the room, Sophia rested her hands on Griffin's cheeks, and Julie watched his eyes well up.

"My dear boy, how I've missed you."

EPILOGUE

One Year Later

A champagne cork popped, and a golden liquid fizzed over the lip of the bottle in the kitchen.

"Congratulations on the newly remodeled place!" Julie's mom called out.

All of Julie and Griffin's guests lifted their glasses with whoops and cheers.

"I can't get over how different this place looks," Angeline said. "With the wall knocked out between the two places, this is practically a mansion."

"It's hardly a mansion, Mom. But thanks. We like it too."

Griffin kissed Julie's forehead and jumped back to his conversation with Uncle Rob about the impending remodel of the ghost tour gift shop. Seeing those two getting along always made her smile.

"Maybe you and Dean can come over for dinner next week after I get back from the speaking engagements in Chicago."

As it turned out, Julie wasn't the only one who'd found someone worth risking the chaos for.

"You're on." Her mom smiled and draped an arm around Julie. "I'm so proud of you, kiddo."

Head resting on her mom's shoulder, Julie watched the most important people in her life mingling in the newly-merged space she and Griffin shared. Wendy and Declan teased each other in the study, where Griffin and Julie's graduate degrees hung side by side amongst an impressive number of old books. Griffin's parents complimented her on the crab dip from the couch that was now just a couch, since Julie and Griffin now had a ghost-free master bedroom to call their very own.

Even Sophia and Francine, the psychic from the day Julie and Griffin met, laughed and made each other ghastly looking cocktails that were at least 75 percent grenadine.

Griffin sauntered over and clasped Julie's hand. Even after all this time, the sight of his smile still gave her that same heady feeling, like falling and flying and a safe place to land all at once.

"Can I borrow you for a second?" he asked.

Julie gave her mom a squeeze before letting Griffin lead her to their balcony. Instead of facing the street, they looked inward at what they'd created together.

"So, how do you like our new home?" Griffin pulled her to him until her back rested on his chest and his solid arms wrapped around her.

"Our home. I like the sound of that." Julie gazed out at the space, now utterly transformed, and couldn't suppress a grin. Julie's old couch, now covered with blankets made by Griffin's grandmother. A new rug and board game table they'd picked out together. The gorgeous built-in bookcase Griffin had made by hand. And best of all, the man beside her who had taught her to embrace the chaos and take a chance on the unknown. Julie's gaze moved to the center shelf where two copies of The Skeptics' Guide nestled together between owl bookends.

"A year ago, who could've predicted all this?" Griffin said.

He kissed her softly.

Over by the cheese dip, Francine snorted, and Sophia winked at Julie.

"Not me. But I like the outcome just the same."

Thank you for reading! For news on new releases, including my new Ghosted paranormal cozy mystery series set in the same world, visit jessicaarden.com or sign up for my newsletter at:

jessicaarden.com/cozynewsletter

Ready for More? Read on for the first chapter of Wendy and Alec's story, *Ghosts of Midnights Past.*

EXCERPT OF GHOSTS OF MIDNIGHTS PAST

New Year's Eve

Early Afternoon

Wendy Deveaux'd had her fill of spirits for the year. Maybe for a whole lifetime, she thought as she guided her last group of tour patrons down St. Peter Street through the throngs of revelers getting an early start on the New Year's festivities. But when your family's in the ghost tour business, spirits are sort of an occupational hazard.

Most of her tour groups were fine, but this afternoon she just couldn't with these people. First, a woman pulled a feint faint outside Hotel Provincial after proclaiming that in a past life she'd seen grisly horrors at the hospital previously on the site. She'd recovered quickly enough after the salt-and-pepper-haired gentlemen she'd been making eyes at since LaFitte's Blacksmith Shop helped her up and offered her the rest of his hurricane. On top of that, Wendy'd also had the joy of not one but three smartasses with bodies of twenty-year olds and senses of humor of twelve-year-old boys. If she heard one more Scooby Doo joke, she was going to do something that would really make them say, "Zoinks." And if anyone else told her she should see that new holiday movie Wings of Love, she was going to lose it.

But they were finally at the last stop. Five more minutes and she was free. She swerved around a group of college-aged girls in sparkly dresses and gathered the group around. Smartass number one made a snide comment and told Wendy to smile. Her urge to punch him in the face was curbed only by a desire not to sully their Yelp rating. She clenched and unclenched her fists. You can do anything for five minutes, Alec used to say. Listen to an awful band, try something new, fall in love.

The unexpected thought of him sent a wistful ache into her chest and stirred up a cocktail of uncomfortable emotions. It snuck up on her like this sometimes. Before her thoughts could wander into areas she'd blocked off with mental caution tape, she shook it off and launched into her final ghostly anecdote about another tragic love story.

Minutes later, after a goodbye and a silent good riddance, Wendy breathed a sigh of relief and forced her aching feet into Deveauxs' Historical Haunts' gift shop. She could use some spirits of the alcoholic variety to celebrate the end of two weeks of triple shifts, but that would have to wait. Her feet might stage a protest if she tried to walk to her car outside the French Quarter before resting for a bit.

Still trying to stave off further thoughts of Alec, she picked up a Voodoo doll key chain that had fallen on the floor. For all the crowds filling the streets talking about New Year's resolutions and drinking themselves to a happy new year, her shop was surprisingly empty save for a few people milling around. The stagnant air of patchouli and sage and dust hit her as she slipped inside—the scent at once comforting and stifling. She ambled down the aisle filled with gris-gris bags, various crystals, and books on French Quarter scandals, and felt her relieved smile fade into a frown. This shop was where her days had begun and ended for as long as she could remember. Everyone else seemed to be making New Year's resolutions and moving along with life, but Wendy was still here. Mostly running the business end of things now that the doctors had ordered her dad to slow down after his bypass surgery, but still in the same place she'd always been.

She stopped to straighten the stand of brochures and business cards on the front counter that separated the store from the offices. Her mood lifted slightly at the sight of the logo and graphics—her own handiwork on display.

Perched on a stool near the register, Wendy's cousin Julie sighed and tapped a pen to her lips.

Wendy's shoulders relaxed a little more at the sight of her best friend and partner in ghost touring. "Ah, the only person I don't want to stab right now. How's the dissertation coming?"

Julie brushed back a curtain of wavy dark brown hair and looked up from her notebook.

"Ugh, don't ask. Slowly," she said, but her expression brightened as she looked up at Wendy. Though Wendy had inherited her mom's fiery auburn hair and fair skin, the Deveaux cousins looked so much alike they were often mistaken for sisters, especially when smirking. They had the same defiant curve to their hips, smart mouths and fondness for tall boots. But while Julie's footwear and demeanor said come hither, Wendy's stompy version warned to proceed with caution.

"Which do you think's a better title?" Julie asked. "Double Homicide, Double Cross, Double Espresso, or Anne Taylor Pantsuit is the New Orange is the New Black: Sophia Durocher's Life In Prison?"

"Definitely the second one." Wendy snorted and grabbed a bottle of water from the fridge behind the counter. "Maybe it wouldn't take so long if you didn't insist on writing everything out longhand."

"Hey, if it was good enough for Dickens and Voltaire, it's good enough for me."

Julie's fiancé Griffin emerged from the stockroom and sauntered up to the counter, his green eyes glinting. "Plus, you can't rush perfection." He set his tool bag down and slipped an arm around Julie's waist. She nuzzled into him.

Wendy rolled her eyes. "I think they can hear my groan in outer space."

But even though she protested, she let a wisp of amusement break through her resting scowl face. Despite her initial reservations about Griffin and her usual dislike of people in general, she had to admit he'd grown on her in the last few years. Sort of. A little.

"What were you doing in the stockroom, anyway?"

"Your dad asked me to fix the shelf that broke."

Wendy frowned. "I was going to do that." Eventually.

"He thought you could use a hand."

Julie set down her pen. "He also said something about how you need to get out of here sometimes. Maybe it was falling asleep in the mashed potatoes that tipped him off."

"Just because I care about our family business succeeding—" Wendy started.

"You are starting to get that eau de patchouli." Julie smelled the air and smirked at her.

Wendy sniffed and folded her arms across her chest, doing a mental calculation of how many hours she'd spent at the shop or doing tours the last three weeks. She'd done all the corporate event tours, all of Norman's tour shifts, and the payroll so Paige could have four days off at Christmas. Her aching calves reminded her she'd walked so much with extra tour shifts, she could probably do the Appalachian Trail without breaking a sweat. Except for the no shower and no restaurant thing. That would be a definite no-go. But still, yeah, she'd been here a lot lately.

"I almost forgot," Julie said, breaking Wendy out of her haze. "Norman and his new girlfriend dropped something off for you." A mischievous smile played at the corners of Julie's mouth, making Wendy's eyes narrow.

Julie reached behind the cash register and produced a forbidding-looking potted plant.

Wendy raised an eyebrow and lifted one of the waxy green mouths that looked like it wanted to bite anything in its path. The corners of her mouth curved upward. She could relate. Perched inside the pot were a craft store pear and a grey plastic bird.

"Aww, a man-eating plant. It looks just like you," Griffin said.

Wendy shot him a glare. "And I was just starting not to hate you."

Julie passed her a card. "This came with it."

Inside, her employee Norman's barely legible handwriting corrected the pre-packaged message.

On the first day of Christmas, my true love third favorite employee gave to me a partridge bird of indeterminate species in a pear tree.

Wendy shook her head, a smile cracking through her fatigue, and she flipped the card open to read the message.

Hey boss,

Thanks for covering my tour shifts all twelve days of Christmas so I could go do this insane thing. Delia says thank you too, by the way. It turns out she's just as cool in person as in the game. And equally hot (and I say that in the most respectful way).

Thanks for pushing me out the door even though it was last minute and not telling me I was crazy. You're the grumpy big sister I never had.

-Norman

Wendy's cold, dead heart swelled a bit. Not that she'd admit it to anyone.

"What's this about?" Julie prodded a plastic cockroach that Wendy had missed inside the flowerpot. Wendy shrugged and shook her head.

"It's Norman. Who knows?"

He was an acquired taste, that was for sure, but Wendy had a soft spot for fellow misfits.

"So I guess things worked out with him and his lady love," Julie said.

"Guess so." Wendy turned back to the pot.

"Good for him," Julie said. "May we all be so bold."

Though it was just an offhand comment, Wendy's eyebrows drew together. The sentiment caused an unexpected stir of discomfort. What would her life be like now if she'd taken a chance and made a different choice?

Until today, she'd successfully pushed off thoughts of Alec for most of the week—probably because she'd been too blissfully busy for her brain to dwell on anything but work, shower, repeat—but even though she'd trained herself to shut down the sentimentality, she couldn't stop a few memories from surfacing now. She remembered the way it felt to wake up next to him, with his sleep mussed hair and the salt and cedar smell of his skin. The notes they'd hidden for each other with the most ridiculous platitudes they could find, like Failure is the condiment that gives success its flavor. The way he would run the gauntlet of her sarcasm to get to what was really underneath. The look in his eyes when she said she wanted to move to Vancouver with him after his assignment here ended. The sound of his voice when she couldn't make herself get on the plane, couldn't leave here after all.

Each thought twisted a knife inside her. There was no use dwelling on this. Stupid sentimental New Year's bullshit. So much of it from her tourists must have rubbed off on her. New Year's resolution—Stop moping around and deal with the choices you've made.

Swallowing around the lump in her throat, Wendy gathered up her Venus flytrap. "We still on for our Doctor Who marathon in a few hours?" she asked Julie. It was their New Year's pre-game tradition to watch a few Christmas specials and drink spiked eggnog before going out.

"You know it." Julie searched her cousin's face and her features clouded with concern.

Wendy tried to rearrange whatever was showing up on her face, with limited success.

"Sure you don't want to go to Miss Peacock's with us after?" Griffin asked. God, even he was being nice to her. She must look awful.

"Come on. Heavy metal mariachis. How can you say no to that?" Julie said.

Wendy sighed. "Oh, I'll find a way."

Once safely in her office, Wendy positioned her new plant on her desk. She collapsed into her chair and rolled her aching shoulders, still trying to shake this pensive state that had so rudely set itself upon her.

Her life was good. Of course it was. She had all of her family close by. She'd been here to step in and run things for her dad after his surgery. Since she'd started booking events and had streamlined some of their systems, their profits had been steadily increasing. Her parents didn't have to worry about medical costs anymore now that she'd taken on a bigger role. That alone was worth it. A small price to pay for not choosing what she wanted.

She pushed a stack of paperwork aside and stretched until her stompy boots clattered onto the desk. She wriggled into her seat and breathed out a sigh. Finally, some time to relax.

But none of the tension flooded from her shoulders. Apparently, her back and spine didn't get the message either.

Wendy muttered a string of expletives and followed the buzzing sound of a fly to where it landed in the mouth of her new carnivorous plant. Maybe Griffin was right—there were four words she never thought she'd say—that it was a rather fitting gift. If anyone dared to get too close, even if Wendy tried to fight against her instinctive reaction, she closed up and they got the business end of her acerbic wit and lifetime of baggage she'd acquired thanks to those awful girls in high school. She scooted closer and watched in morbid fascination as the fly wandered around the pinkish plant mouth. The thing was a minefield of tiny translucent hair triggers. One wrong step, and...Wendy's shoulders tensed even further at the impending doom playing out before her. But seconds ticked by and nothing happened. Huh.

Maybe this was some kind of vegetarian flytrap, an evolved sort that had figured out a way to circumvent its baser instincts.

Maybe she could figure out a way to do the same.

But just as she entertained the notion, the jaws snapped shut. Despite its frantic buzzing, the poor fly was trapped.

It got what was coming to it for chancing an encounter with a prickly plant.

A few minutes later, once Wendy had distracted herself with a cup of tea, Griffin poked his head around the doorframe.

"What?" she asked, with more bite in her voice than she'd intended.

He held up a folded note. "I almost forgot. I found this in the storage room."

Wendy's vision telescoped in on her name written in Alec's steady handwriting. Her breath stilled. Time seemed to go sideways at the sight of this artifact from the past. They'd probably left hundreds of these for each other over the course of their relationship. Never gushy, just silly things to make each other laugh, like Shoot for the stars. Even if you miss, you might hit a bird. Or The early bird gets the breakfast burrito. How long had that been here, hiding amongst the boxes of brochures and ghost shot glasses? How many more of these time bombs were out there? Grenades to the heart.

Julie appeared by Griffin's side and looked from the note to Wendy, eyes widening in recognition. "I'll take care of that." She snapped it up.

Wendy's stomach clenched. Why did a simple note from him affect her so much? Even when they hadn't seen each other in nine months. Especially after she was the one who couldn't get past her fears and had walked away.

She shifted in her seat. She should just let Julie take it and throw it away and try to focus on—what exactly? More work? More spreadsheets and group events. She was already set for the next two weeks. Stress knitting a new sweater? Her gaze landed on the novel jutting out of her purse. The graphic she was making for her friend Autumn's book! Yes, that was something happy to focus on. See, she was going to be just fine.

But as Julie tucked the note into her pocket, the hollowed-out part of Wendy's heart felt scraped raw. Maybe the schlocky sentiment of this time of year was getting to her, or maybe she was just a glutton for punishment.

"No." Wendy held out her hand. "I'll take it."

"Are you sure?" Julie held the note to her chest, and her features etched with concern.

Before she could change her mind, Wendy nodded.

"We're going to get out of here, but Paige is holding down the fort in the shop until your parents and Rayjay get here," Julie said after reluctantly relinquishing the note. "See you at your place in an hour?" Her eyes searched Wendy's for any sign she needed immediate backup. "Or I can wait, and we can grab a ride together."

Wendy gave Julie her best I'm fine smile and shooed her cousin and Griffin away. "Get out of here before you smell like patchouli, too."

Once they left, Wendy pulled her office door shut and returned to her desk. She picked up the note and rubbed her thumb over the year-old ink like she could somehow transport herself back to the time that was populated by private jokes and cheesy movies, and someone to dress up with at comic conventions. To a time when she'd somehow made it work. He'd calmed her suspicions, and she'd finally let him in. She missed him so much it hurt.

She lifted the corner of the paper, and at the sight of more of his handwriting and what looked like a drawing, resistance slammed into her.

It was only a few lines of text from days gone by. But it was also a Pandora's box of what-ifs.

What if she hadn't been so sure he'd eventually walk away? What if she hadn't been so chickenshit? Would she change things if she could go back and do it all over again?

Well, that was dumb to even consider because of course she couldn't.

She could call him, though. She could try to apologize again. Explain. He'd shot her down the first time after she realized the colossal mistake she'd made, but after all this time, he'd listen even if he was still hurt and angry. She knew him well enough to know that. There was a good chance he was even in town right now. The thought that he was here and not with her tugged at her. He might even find it in his heart to give her another chance.

But she knew herself too well, too. No matter how hard she fought against it, maybe it would always just be a matter of time before she panicked and shut him out again. And there was no way she'd do that to him a second time. Not if she wasn't absolutely sure she could stick it out despite the chance of being hurt. She cared about him too much.

But if she could do that.... She turned the note over in her hands. Her heart did a little skip, but then she looked at her new plant and frowned.

Right. That was about as likely as getting Prince to come back from the dead for a revival performance.

Wendy set the note back down on her desk unread.

Maybe it was time she started looking forward instead of back.

When Wendy finally felt like her legs wouldn't turn to Jell-O if she took another step, she poked her head out of her office. "Heading out?" Paige asked from behind the register.

"I'm going to see if we need anything else and restock the beads first," Wendy said. "Unless you need me."

"Nah, I got this." Paige repinned a loose blond strand that had fallen out of her ponytail. "So have you got any big New Year's plans now that you finally have a night off?" Paige said once the customers had left.

Wendy shrugged. "Just hanging out with Julie this afternoon. I'll probably fall asleep on my feet after that."

"I get that. Hey, have you seen that new holiday movie, Wings of Love? You should check that out if you get time this week."

Wendy stewed. This was the big schlocky second chance miracles block-buster. There would be no second chances for her. It was pretty hard to come back from promising to move to Vancouver with someone and then not getting on the plane and breaking things off instead.

"Why does everyone think I need to see this sappy movie?" Wendy snapped. "You're like the eighth person today who's told me to watch it."

Paige gave her a confused look. "It's not sappy. It's about a back-up dancer turned climate scientist reunited with her lost love, the Prime Minister of Cana-da. They're stuck on a plane together circling the North Pole when elves attack. Sort of the Snakes on a Plane of holiday movies. But weirdly poignant at the end," she said. "Totally your kind of thing."

"Oh."

"And it has Will Morton."

"Well, maybe then." Wendy gave a half smile. Paige was just being nice. But planes, cheesy movies that were exactly her thing—her and Alec's thing—it was hard not to feel like the universe had planned every detail of this day to taunt her with reminders of Alec and how everyone else was making resolutions and traveling to new countries and trying new recipes and here she was, mired in the same place she'd always been.

"Your parents and Rayjay are coming in an hour, and Norman said to call him for backup if we needed another hand. And don't worry about the beads. I can do that later."

Wendy grunted her assent, sounding more like her father than she liked. She grabbed her purse and took a few steps toward the door, but when she spotted the anemic-looking bead rack, she doubled back to the storeroom. They'd probably be busy later. Best to get them stocked up, in case there was a rush before the night crew got there.

She was elbow-deep in a box of purple and green Mardi Gras throws when footsteps approached, and she anticipated Paige's protests. "I know. I know." She hung gold beads with attached shot glasses. "But really, I can't in good conscience leave you like this with a mob of drunken people who want their beads."

But instead of Paige's cheerful chirp, a low, soothing voice from Wendy's past stilled her hands on the rack. "Good to know you're still looking out for me."

Plastic beads clanged together. Heat and cold flashed inside her chest at the achingly familiar sound. Slowly, she straightened the last necklace and turned around, half convinced she was hallucinating from lack of sleep. But no.

"Alec," she breathed. He smiled his familiar smile, one side of his mouth tilted upward and a single dimple formed in his cheek. Dark brown curls fell just above his eyes and he fixed his steady gaze on her.

"Happy almost New Year," he said.

Words deserted her. Like she'd somehow conjured him, he was here. Her Alec who said "aboot" instead of about and serviette instead of napkin and gave her a run for her money at Trivial Pursuit. The same Alec who made her laugh and went out of his way to be kind to people others made fun of. Alec who ate hot sauce on everything and had to drink Red Bull to stay up past 11p.m.. She took in all six foot something of him standing there before her in dark jeans and a henley that looked so worn and soft that she had to fight the urge to touch him. The heather of his shirt made his sea glass eyes lean more blue than green. The fanciful parts of her—who knew those existed?—danced around like this was some sort of fucking sign, and she immediately put the smack down on that line of thinking. But... but part of her wanted to lay her head on his chest and breathe in the wintry aftershave scent of him and give up the fight that was always raging inside of her, warning her to keep her distance, keep vigilant.

"I've missed this place." His gaze flicked around the store, but settled firmly back on Wendy, roaming her face in a way that felt like he was memorizing every detail. The thrum in her chest edged out all other sounds. Easy. Do not get so excited. "I saw the new sign out front. You design that?"

She moved her eyes to the ground to steady herself and nodded.

"I like it. Still has the same charm as the old one, but looks like it will last."

"Thanks. That's what I was going for."

Alec toyed with one of the strands of beads on the shelf, and it felt for a moment like he'd never left, like he would always be a part of this place.

"You just missed Julie and Griffin."

"Ah, too bad. I would've liked to catch up with them, too."

What was she supposed to do here? She hadn't planned for a mini reunion. This was all uncharted territory.

"What are you doing here?" Wendy finally sputtered.

"I spent the holidays with my sister," he said. "I'm flying out tonight on a red-eye."

"I thought you might have." Wendy swallowed, her palms growing slick. She gathered her courage because she had to know. "But why are you here?"

He met her eyes, and a charge went through her like the electricity in the air before a coming storm.

No. No. No. This was a bad idea. She should send him on his way. Save them both the heartache.

"I wanted to see you, see how you were doing." Alec's gaze moved toward her office. "Could we talk?"

Bad idea. Abort. Abort.

"Sure."

Get Ghosts of Midnights Past at jessicaarden.com

ACKNOWLEDGEME|

The week before this novella was originally published as a part of the Under Your Spell boxed set, I sat down to write a thank you to the people who made this book possible. As I reflected and drafted, I found myself overcome with gratitude. I've been surrounded by the best people I could possibly imagine, from the early and enduring support from my parents who sparked my lifelong love of stories to the teachers, mentors, writing partners, friends and family. You've asked about my work, helped me through early drafts, and commiserated with me over chocolate and wine,

First, thank you to my family. My parents and in-laws have been the best anyone could ask for. Mom, I'll always remember reading with you as a child and your constant encouragement and allowance to seek out books. You started this, and I'm glad. My siblings, Jenny, Laure, Nate, and my siblings-in-law, Michael and Jenny have been a constant source of encouragement. This book (or any other) wouldn't exist without my mother-in-law, Judy, who saved my sanity many times by taking care of the boys so I could write or go to critique group nights. She gave me the gift of time to nurture what was important to me, and I am endlessly grateful.

Thank you also to Miriam Salas Orta for hosting us in New Orleans when I did research for this book and to Alysia Cox and Debi Spencer for help with forensic questions.

My various writer groups and friends have been a source of education and camaraderie, particularly the LVRWA, the NBC writers and my favorite Face-book-group-that-shall-not-be-named with copious amounts of smart writer talk, Idris Elba and Justin Trudeau—you know who you are. And you are awesome.

I'm also incredibly grateful to early readers, copy editors, and proofreader who helped shape Julie and Griffin's story: Sheryl Greenblatt (my long-time critique partner, sounding board, and general sanity keeper), Jennifer Sable, Karen Jagi, Amanda Denning, G.G. Andrew, Amanda Gale, Saskia Blake, Nicole Zoltak, Elizabeth Cole, and Bryn Donovan. An extra special thanks to Bryn, who took the helm of the Under Your Spell anthology project and the whole group of writers who were a part of it with me. Working with you all was a pleasure.

And finally, thanks to my husband Paul and my two boys. Thanks for being by my side. Paul, you are my rock. Thanks for pushing me when I need pushing, giving me new perspectives and cheering me on , even when I closed up and got scared of being vulnerable. You kept us fed when I was up until 2am writing to meet my deadlines. Thank you for being in this and in everything else with me.

About the Author

Jessica Arden writes cozy mysteries, and quirky contemporary romance, usually with a supernatural twist. She's stomped grapes in her native California, hiked 350 miles on an ancient pilgrimage route in Spain, had breakfast with a coatimundi in Costa Rica, and spent the night in a monastery. But no matter where life takes her, her true north will always be with her husband and two energetic boys.

When she's not writing, you can find Jessica teaching college English classes, designing graphics, logos, and book covers, making crafts, reading and watching way too much TV.

ALSO BY JESSICA ARDEN

Romance

The Skeptics' Guide to Love Duet

The Skeptics' Guide to the Mysteries of the Universe (Book 1)

Ghosts of Midnights Past (Book 2)

Stand Alones

Vegas Strong Collection

Collide

Cozy Mystery

The Ghosted Cozy Mystery Series

Once Ghosted, Twice Shy (Book 1)